W9-BXE-399

KILLING TIME IN CRYSTAL CITY

ALSO BY CHRIS LYNCH

Angry Young Man

Freewill

Gypsy Davey

Iceman

Inexcusable

Kill Switch

Little Blue Lies

Pieces

Shadow Boxer

CHRIS LYNCH

KILLING TIME IN CRYSTAL CITY

SIMON & SCHUSTER BFYR
New York London Toronto Sydney New Delhi

An imprint of Simon & Schuster Children's Publishing Division
1230 Avenue of the Americas, New York, New York 10020

For information about special discounts for bulk purchases, please contact Simon & Schuster Special Sales at 1-866-506-1949 or business@simonandschuster.com.
The Simon & Schuster Speakers Bureau can bring authors to your live event.
For more information or to book an event, contact
the Simon & Schuster Speakers Bureau at 1-866-248-3049
or visit our website at www.simonspeakers.com.
Jacket design by Krista Vossen
Interior design by Hilary Zarycky
The text for this book is set in Berling.
Manufactured in the United States of America
2 4 6 8 10 9 7 5 3 1
Library of Congress Cataloging-in-Publication Data
Lynch, Chris.
Killing time in Crystal City / Chris Lynch. — 1st edition.
pages cm
Summary: Seventeen-year-old Kevin tries to reinvent himself when he runs away from home and the father he hates, but living with a mysterious uncle and befriending two homeless girls just adds more complications.
ISBN 978-1-4424-4011-1 (hardcover) — ISBN 978-1-4424-4013-5 (eBook)
[1. Runaways—Fiction. 2. Homeless persons—Fiction. 3. Fathers and sons—Fiction. 4. Uncles—Fiction. 5. Family problems—Fiction.] I. Title.
PZ7.L979739Kin 2015
[Fic]—dc23
2013043299

KILLING TIME IN CRYSTAL CITY

DEPARTURE

I came for the name.

I should probably be embarrassed to admit making a big decision based on such lameness. But I figure if you are aiming for a place to do a total reboot on your whole entire self, then you aim for a place with a name like Crystal City.

It's a name that calls you to come. As soon as you see it on a map, or on a bus schedule, or if you hear somebody mention it, the impulse is to think, yup, that's the place. It wants me and I want it. It conjures immediately *The* Crystal City, the very home of clarity and radiance and shimmering promise. I can't be the only one to have noticed that. I know. So it has to attract lots of people, peoples, types. Lots of people who are looking for stuff. Looking for what I'm looking for.

Whatever that turns out to be.

More than anything, it needs to *not* be the place I am leaving behind. Ass Bucket is the name of my town. Not really. But, really.

I might well find out what I *am* looking for just by going. Maybe somebody there will even tell me.

Or, possibly, I don't have to wait that long.

She gets on the bus at our one stopover, the midpoint between Ass Bucket and Crystal City. I wouldn't have noticed her, since I have the premium, top-deck, front-seat position, except that she bangs her way up the stairs and down the aisle with the kind of stomp and thump that just forces you to turn and look.

So I turn and look.

She throws her backpack onto the window seat and takes the aisle seat, second from rear, left. I become aware of my staring only when she stares back, with an exaggerated head tilt and a dropped open mouth that are not meant to flatter me.

She has *noticed* me. Already, right there, my life has changed beyond all recognition.

She has a cast on her left arm. I have a cast on my right. If you do not answer when the universe calls out to you as clearly as that then you, pal, are a shitbag and you deserve to be a shitbag and live the loser life that comes with it.

I turn away and look at the road ahead, because she intimidated me and forced me to. But every real part of me wants to do the opposite, wants to do what I would never do. Before, anyway. I would never make that long and scary walk down that aisle separating me from her. Before.

Now, however, I can't stop thinking about doing exactly that. The road and the cars and the landscape ahead, so mesmerizing up till now, are suddenly nothing, and the girl behind me means everything. If I can't do this now, when everything tells me this is the this and now is the now, then I might as well just slither out the bus window and walk all the way back to Ass Bucket to resume my former life as a shitbag.

That thought propels me out of my seat, onto my feet, backpack in tow, to my new best seat in the house. Aisle seat, second from rear, right.

I sit for ten silent minutes, which is not really that long of a silence unless every one of those six hundred seconds is spent on my agonizing over coming up with an opening, *the* opening, that will launch the conversation and the future and all the incredible betters and bests waiting for me in that future, and an eleventh minute waterlogged in the realization that the reason I am speechless is that I have just put *all* that lifetime of pressure on this one small opening jab of communication.

Just speak, ya dope.

"We have something in common," I say, shocked at the sound of my own voice but not as shocked as I am at the sight and sensation of reaching boldly across the aisle and tapping her cast with mine. I draw my arm rapidly back to my territory and savor the sad and thrilling reverberation of that instant of human contact, and plaster be damned because human contact it was.

She turns her head slowly in my direction, the kind of slowly that suggests I'm either getting attitude already or maybe her neck was also injured in whatever accident did her arm harm. I'm hoping the universe doesn't hold it against me that I am wishing her neck pain over attitude.

The long turn of her head takes a little detour to look at the spot where I touched her—like I left a stain or something—then continues up to engage my actual face.

"What?" she says. Could she possibly know of the torture that went into the first run of my clever line, never mind the rerun?

"I said, we have something in common," I say, and watch with fascination as this arm, which apparently belongs to me but could just as easily be the mechanical grabber on one of those carnival claw machines, reaches over and taps hers again.

"Well, it wouldn't be *proper boundaries*, because *I* have them. I also have pepper spray, a knife, and steel-toed boots I like to call the 'testicle testers.'"

This is not how it's supposed to go. The new and wider and bolder world is supposed to be friendlier and appreciate gestures like this. I am supposed to get things *right* this time. And the new and wider and bolder me cannot just accept this kind of failure if things are going to improve, and they *have to improve, they have to improve.*

"I'm sorry," I say, leaning in a slightly unnatural way in the opposite direction from her. And I place my left hand on top of my casted right forearm, as if I can hide the shameful thing.

I cannot possibly hold this pitiful and awkward posture for the rest of the ride, but I fear I am going to attempt it, shitbag that I am.

Fortunately, I don't have to put it to the test because after about two minutes, she speaks to me.

"Hey," she says, and I turn cautiously to see her expression not quite the hard thing it was. Her face shows what I might possibly recognize as pity, which I am more than happy to accept.

"What?" I say. I try to match the disinterested tone she used when she asked me that same question, because I think that acting the way this cool person does is a pretty good step to start on whatever it is I'm starting on. She doesn't seem to notice.

"How'd you get yours?" she asks, pointing from within her proper boundary area at my cast.

Oh. Oh right. What kind of feeb am I, that I thought I could initiate an arm-cast discussion that wouldn't come fairly quickly to this question, which I do not want to answer? Which I really, really, do not want to answer.

"My dad did it." The words burst out of me like the stream from one of those pump-action water guns.

"Oh," she says, but an unstartled "oh." "You poor kid."

She doesn't follow it up for any elaboration, which is a surprise and a relief.

"How about you?" I say, pointing from an appropriate distance because already I'm learning these rules of the road I'll need to live by.

"What? I don't even know you. I'm not telling you something like that."

What? That was an option? Opting out was an option?

"I didn't know that was an option. Just refusing to answer the question? Especially after you just . . . that's an option?"

She tilts her head again, befuddled by my befuddlement. We've only just met but this is already an unfortunate recurring motif in our relationship. She knows I'm a dolt before she knows my name.

"Everything is an option. Nobody has to say or not say anything they don't want to. Don't you know even that much?"

"Of course I do. I was just . . . I was going by what you . . .

I'm trying to work out the way things are done. . . ." The trailing off at the end is the most intelligent part of my response.

"Did the spaceship forget to come back for you?"

"Hnn. Yeah. Very funny. Actually, I'm just out, seeing the world."

She's underimpressed. "Right, well maybe you should think about going back home," she says with a drop of kindness that unsettles me. "I'd worry that you're going to struggle at this."

Home. Where is that? *What* is that? I'm happy to go there, but all I know for sure is that whatever home is, for me it's not *back* anywhere, it's someplace out forward.

"What *this* is it that I'm going to struggle at?" I ask, still undecided about what percentage impressed/offended I am at what she's thinking she's knowing about me.

"Running away," she says with a dollop of *duh* in her voice.

"I'm not running away from anything," I say. I hope I sound more like an appalled man than a cornered six-year-old, but I wouldn't bet money on it.

"Okay," she says, shrugging. "But I'd still be worried that maybe the street could be an unkinder place to an innocent somebody than home. Even a home with an arm-breaking father in it. What does your mother think about it all?"

I am trying to work out how she does this, slipping

multiple provocations into such brief strings of sentences. What would be the *it all* that this *mother* would have an opinion on? *Innocent somebody*, by the way? *The street?* What and where is this street, and what does it have to do with me at all?

"Why would I tell you that?" I say. "I don't even know you. I don't have to answer that."

She laughs, deep and rich like a hot hearty soup, and I notice her left eyetooth is missing. "Okay," she says, "so it's possible that you are capable of learning some things as you go along. You might not be quite hopeless."

Now we're getting someplace. She's already easier for me to talk to. So I go for it.

"You're coming on to me now, aren't you."

She tilts her head this time at such an unfeasible angle it could possibly twist right off.

"Right, well, I knew this was your first time running away, but I didn't realize it was your first time ever leaving the house."

"It's not," I blurt far too quickly in my desperation to quash the idea.

She laughs harder this time. "You actually responded to that. That is so cute."

"It isn't," I say, tragically persevering.

She turns away from me, from my overwhelming cute

imbecility that might be contagious. She looks like she's addressing me in my original seat way up there at the front and the top of the bus, back in that time when the only fully developed idea I had about proceeding to better things was that the top and the front of everything were what you should always shoot for.

"You're giving me a real dilemma here, funny boy. I should throw you back like the little fish you are, except that you've already amused me more than anybody has amused me in a long time."

The fact that I have been inadvertently amusing does not have to be a problem for anybody.

"You're welcome."

"And what little conscience I still have is nagging at me not to let you go out there and get savaged by all the big fish waiting just for you."

She's doing it again with the provocations.

"Hey," I snap, or nearly snap anyway, but do enunciate clearly and with vigor. "Who asked you to do anything? I don't think I at any point suggested that I needed you to *let* me or not let me go *out there*, even if such a place as *out there* actually existed or represented a challenge that I was unprepared to meet."

She hesitates several seconds, continuing to stare ahead, composing herself, then turns to me, smiling broadly. "Oh, it does. And you are. And you're doing it again, being kind of adorable and I think I just might be in love."

I have my righteous scolding finger already poised, and my mouth open to retort when her words themselves finish the long journey to my brain and I jam to a halt.

"Oh," she says, pointing at my face. "First thing, right away, you're going to have to lose that blushing thing or you are dead meat out there. And God, boy, if that means you took the love thing literally, then man oh man do we have our work cut out for us."

Ah, crap.

"I'll take the rapid blinking to mean, unfortunately, yes."

"Grrr," I say, punching my own thigh with my cast. "How can I possibly have the option not to answer something if my face keeps answering for me?"

"No doubt about it, you've got a conundrum there. A poker face is probably one of those things that you have to grow, over time, like a beard. Hey, maybe grow a beard."

"Yeah, thanks, but if you look closely I think you'll agree that beard-growing is another thing you could probably do better than me."

It appears I have said something wrong.

"What?" I say. "What? I was talking about my *inability* to grow a beard, not your *ability* to. Come on, you don't have a beard."

"Yes, I do."

"No, you don't."

"Yes, I do, and thank you for pointing it out, zithead."

"Ah, so it's my skin now. Very nice. Feels like I'm talking to my sister."

"So, you have a sister, then."

"Grrrr. No, I don't."

"Does she have a beard? Is she in the circus?"

"Can we start over again?" I say, with prayer-hands for emphasis.

"Why? This was just getting fun."

"Fun is overrated."

"That's extremely sad," she says in an extremely sad tone. "Just how bad was your father?"

This one's easy. "I don't want to talk about that."

"Okay. Then how 'bout, what's your name?" She extends her healthy right hand to me across the aisle.

I happily extend my less-healthy one across to her. Finally, a question I am not only anxious to answer, but one I have prepped for.

"Kiki Vandeweghe." Because why not, right?

She splutters a laugh right in my face, but still shakes my hand.

"Your name is Kiki Vandeweghe."

"That is correct."

"I was going to guess Benedict, or Kenton, or Skippy."

"Kiki Vandeweghe," I assure her.

"And you're just gonna go with that, yeah?"

"Because it's my name."

"Your very red ears wiggle a bit when you lie. Awfully cute. Like how elephants flap away overheating with their ears."

"Kiki. Van—"

"Where have I heard that name before? Is it some sports—"

"So what's your name?" I blurt.

She laughs. "Well, I was gonna be Kiki Vandeweghe until you showed up. So I guess I'll go with Anastasia Dimbleby."

"Really?" I say, as if anybody's name should really come as a surprise.

"For you, we'll just leave it at Stacey. Best not to make things any more complicated for you than they already are."

Right, so it's more mockery. No problem. "Thanks for that, Stacey," I say, getting a stupid little shot of thrill when I say her name.

Stacey. My friend, Stacey. I made a friend. Already.

"What are you, like a human thermometer or something?" she says. "You need to get that blushing thing checked before your head pops right off."

I really, really do, dammit.

"Sign?" I say, pulling out the little stubby blue marker that I have been carrying for just this purpose.

"What?"

"I want you to sign my cast. I want to collect signatures as a kind of record of my travels. And then I'll sign yours."

"Okay," she says, shrugging, "but no thanks on signing mine. I prefer all record of my travels to be kept inside my head and no place else." She then goes on to sign "Anastasia Dimbleby" in long sloppy script along the belly of the forearm part. I'm about to pull back when she turns it over and signs "Stacey" across the knuckle part where I can look at it all the time.

"So, Stacey, are you running away?"

"Why would I do that? I don't run away from things, things run away from me. I'm just on a kind of grand tour."

"That sounds nice," I say.

"Nice," she repeats, but in a tone with twelve more layers of everything than the one I used.

"When did the tour start?"

"Two and a half years ago."

"When does it finish?"

She lets this last one sit there for several seconds, though her face shows nothing along the lines of pondering.

"I haven't given that a single minute of thought."

That one sounds like a hint that further questions will not be taken at this time. So we both just look ahead for now.

• • •

There it is. I can see it coming, and I rush back up through the near-empty bus to my original seat so I can take it all in fully.

Crystal City.

"Don't you want to come up here and have a look, Stacey?" I call back to her. Best seats in the house. She has her eyes closed and waves at me wearily. I return to the view by myself.

Is there a better capsule, a better pod of motion and vision? A space module, sure, I'd be on that right now if it was ever on offer, pointing and laughing at everybody stuck down here on Planet Puke. But let's be real. And real is the front seat on the top deck of a bus going *somewhere.* Everything is in front, everything's forward. Nothing's behind you, no rear window view for you, sir.

The bus station I come into, though, looks just like the bus station I pulled out of. Could just about be the same place. Could be a big fat fast one played on me, and the driver took a big wobbly go-round to get back to the same, same place.

Except why would he do that? Because people don't need reasons. Making believe that people need reasons to be demented and shitty accomplishes nothing other than to make you demented and shitty yourself. Which you don't want. I have to remember to tell Stacey that at an appropriate moment so she knows that I did in fact learn a little something about life before I met her. A little something.

Except, anyway, I saw it, more than the bus station. I saw Crystal City on the approach. So no matter how much the travel zombie industry wants to disguise their zombie-town depots to look just like each other everywhere, we know better. We won't fall for it, because we have arrived, and we know it.

Why do they want to do that anyway, make your destination look like your departure when they know all you want to do with your departure point is to depart it?

Anyway.

"Anyway," I say, as the bus hisses into its bay and I return to collect my backpack and my actual friend.

The bus station of Crystal City is precisely as grimy as the one back in Ass Bucket. It's a little bigger, though, so there are more bays, more buses coming in, more going out, belching more exhaust into the oily air and beeping randomly and for no apparent reason other than to make everybody more jaggedy and angry.

I follow behind Stacey as we bump our way out of the big daytime dusk of the garage area, fighting through the flow of fellow travelers to get to the terminal on the other side of the thick glass doors. Already my eyes feel irritated and what passes for air here is working my lungs over to provoke the first whistlings of wheeze as I breathe.

The diesel-mechanical stench is replaced by a deep-fried-humanity stench as we push through the doors into the waiting lounge, cafeteria, ticketing offices tilt-a-whirl of busfolk society. Just a few steps in, Stacey turns around sharply and I almost bump into her before braking.

"Is that you making that noise?" she says.

"No," I say, and lung-whistle right through it.

"Of course," she says. "Of course you have asthma. Why wouldn't you have asthma?"

"Okay," I say firmly, "first, it's *controlled* asthma, it's only that the concentrated bus fumes set it off a little. And second, is that some kind of asthmatic stereotyping thing you're doing there? Because that would be very uncool."

Stacey's hungry grin tells me that my passionate defense of the maligned tribe of asthma sufferers has done nothing to the old fire of prejudice other than throw another log onto it. Before she can say more, however, she's cut off.

"Derek?" says the small, nerved-up girl who nudges Stacey aside to speak right into my chin like it's a microphone. "Are you Derek? You are, right? Sure, it *is* you. It's me, Molly." As she says her name she smiles really hard, really hard, as if you can amp up a smile like you can a scream. She also holds up her right arm, showing me her cast.

Her intensity could just about push me backward all by itself but I help it along by inching away from her breath, which is slightly sour but with a top layer of Scope that is so strong it's almost a mist.

"Sorry," I say, "but I'm not Derek."

"What?" she says, sounding genuinely perplexed by my failure to be Derek. "But you look like you, pretty much. And it's the time, and I'm here. And the cast, and everything. You have the cast, and everything."

Stacey takes this as her cue, and bumps Molly's shoulder with a casted forearm roughly enough to send her sideways into the path of a big fat businessguy, who jolts her even harder without seeming to notice.

"Yo, rudegirl," Stacey says as Molly pushes her glasses back up her face and fails to hide the large, watering eyes. "You are mistaken. This is Kiki Vandeweghe, he's not your Derek."

I'm looking at the slight, twitchy girl whose voice sounds like she has an air bubble trapped in her throat, and who is dealing with the superior force that is Stacey by wrapping her arms around one another in what looks like a badly needed hug. And as I'm looking I think I am sorry for not being Derek. I'm sorry I couldn't have been that, and prevented this.

"Hey, sorry," Stacey says a lot more warmly now that she

has made her point about manners and now that she can see the delicacy of the little lost creature before her. "Are you all right? Are you hurt?"

Molly shakes her head without speaking and continues her unilateral embrace. Her hair is a large gingery mass of a garden with curly parts and frizzy parts and bushy parts shaped into an almost perfect globe. She seems to have attempted some kind of parting in there between the middle and the left side but it's mostly fought back, and the overpowered hair clip is really just floating about six inches away from the scalp. Between the shape, the color, and the midstripe it looks a lot like a Cleveland Browns helmet.

Stacey steps up to her and gently takes the clip, which appears to be in the form of a yellow school bus, and works it back through the hair to where it belongs. Molly holds completely still, but follows Stacey intently with her wide eyes.

Suddenly it occurs to me. Maybe I just could be Derek. *The* Derek or *a* Derek, what's the difference? I'm betting no difference at all, as far as Molly is concerned. So yeah, why not? She could have her Derek, the universe could have some rightness, and I'm pretty sure it would even be okay with Kiki since he is currently unattached.

"What's this, a convention or somethin'?"

Startled, I look to my left where the speaker is holding up a left arm almost completely covered in a cast that is bent at the elbow. Since it is twice the cast of anybody else's here, I'm thinking he may want to be our leader.

"No, it's not a convention," is my clever response to the man who acknowledges me not at all.

"Molly?" he says, walking right up to Stacey. "Please, tell me you're Molly."

Stacey goes right on taking care of the business of hairdressing before she sizes the guy up. "Even if I was Molly, I wouldn't tell you I was Molly."

Molly tells him she is Molly anyway. "I'm Molly."

Stacey is still looking the guy up and down when she says to her, "Are you sure? Maybe you're not Molly."

"I'm Derek," he says, still staring at Stacey and staring a stare that says he is failing to recognize any of the hostility waves radiating from her.

I step in quickly. "Sign my cast, Derek?"

"What?" he snaps, but grabs the marker and squiggles his mark along the outer edge up near the elbow.

"This is your Derek?" Stacey asks, getting in between them and holding her gaze.

"I guess so," Molly says.

"Who are you?" Derek asks Stacey's back. Stacey's back keeps him on hold.

"You thought he"—she thumb-points back at Derek—"looked like him?" She pinkie-points at me.

"The picture was kinda blurry," Molly says, the air bubble in her throat expanding.

"Oh, the picture is more than *kinda* blurry," Stacey says.

"What picture are we talking about?" I ask.

"Uh, I'm here to meet Molly, right, so if the two of you who are not Molly would be on your way, we can get on with getting to know each other."

"*That* picture," Stacey snaps.

And a picture he is. I mean, I know I'm not bringing home any blue ribbons from the fair, but if he looks like me it has to be me after being dragged underneath a truck, left to age in the summer sun for a couple of months, and then given an all-over coating of a fine-grade motor oil. Although, it appears by his dense stubble that he is well capable of growing a beard. Like, three times a day.

"How old are you, *De-rek*?" Stacey says with a hammer blow to that second syllable.

He seems to be up for the game with her, which I personally think is unwise.

"Why don't we just call it early thirties," he says, all leery.

"What piss," Stacey spits. "I didn't ask what year you were *born*."

"See, Molly," Derek says, leaning in to take her hand, "I tried to be nice and get along with your friends, for your sake, but it just doesn't work with some people."

Then, it goes emphatically wrong.

Then, Molly *takes his hand*.

Then, Stacey nearly takes *off* Molly's hand, in slapping the two apart.

"What's *wrong* with you, girl?" Stacey says, starting to shuffle the girl away toward the streetside exit. "This is a bad thing. You have to know this is a bad thing."

"Nothing's wrong with me," Molly says, but puts up no resistance to Stacey's mothering.

"You are outta line," Derek snarls, walking after them. "She wants to be with me."

Even though nobody's invited me, I start fast-walking after them. Derek is managing a seriously quick stride that keeps pace with the now-running girls while at the same time not looking like he's chasing or pursuing anybody. The kind of thing I'd think takes practice.

What kind of guy practices that?

Myself, I'm pretty sure I look like I'm running, or run-shambling, as I catch up to the action. The girls have reached and gone through the middle one of a five-across bank of glass doors to the street. They run hard left. Seconds later, Derek goes through that same door while I pass through the one to his immediate left.

Then it all becomes a mess of a run-shamble as I half-stumble, half-throw myself to the ground in Derek's path. I fall hard to the pavement, breaking my fall mostly with my good arm while I also take Derek right out of the play. He hits my side just below his knees and just like that he is up and over, his legs taken right out from under him. I am looking in the direction of the fleeing girls as Derek flies over me and hits the pavement with his jaw after his big bent cast breaks all up on impact with the sidewalk.

He is howling and growling, rolling on the ground and holding his resmashed broken arm and bleeding a good puddle from his mouth as I scramble up and scram away.

I might not be a superhero, but I can fall down like nobody's business.

I walk up the street, through the center of Crystal City, trying to catch up to them. I trot for a couple of blocks and then walk hard for a couple more. Then I walk slowly for a couple more, before I start trying side streets off the main drag and then side streets off those, with no plan, no idea what I'm doing. And no luck.

ONCE THERE WAS JASPER

"How did you get this way?" Jasper asked me, about a week before the school year ended. Or the quarter year for me since I only moved after the April vacation. We were walking the six miles home from school, because it was a Thursday. We walked home Tuesdays and Thursdays. That was Jasper's idea because he said it made the weeks shorter.

I never felt it did any such thing. Nothing made the weeks shorter. But I walked with him every Tuesday and Thursday because if I didn't he would just walk on without me, and then where would I be?

Jasper was my friend. He was my best friend. As well as my second-, third-, and fourth-best friend.

Jasper was also genius at conceiving questions that served no purpose other than to drive me demented. "See, I know where this goes," I said. "First, I'm expected to say, 'What way?' Because then you get to tell me how screwed up I am before then going on to get me to list the reasons why. As if I agree with you in the first place, which I don't. But you can just forget about it, because I'm short-circuiting your whole plan by not asking what you mean by 'this way.'"

It was a disused railway line, this long Tuesday-Thursday walk we took. Lots of overgrown grass. When he was bored, Jasper would make various train noises, and my favorite was the low and rhythmic *chunk-chunk, chunk-chunk, chunk-chunk* of the cars rolling over the seams in the track.

"*Chunk-chunk,*" he said, then, "*chunk-chunk, chunk-chunk . . .*"

"You can *chunk*-chunk all you want, but I'm not going to ask."

"You sound ridiculous. The accent is on the second *chunk*."

"I'm still not going to ask."

"Of course you're not . . . *chunk-chunk, chunk-chunk* . . . because you know very well how you are."

Sometimes they didn't even have to be questions and they would wind me up anyway.

"No, wise guy. Actually, I don't."

"No? Okay, then, let me tell you. You're kind of paranoid. You're a doomsayer."

"I'm not a doomsayer."

"Oh yes. You are a sayer of doom. And self-pitying. You're Olympic-standard at making yourself out to be the victim in everything."

"Stop picking on me."

"Ha. Good one."

"Good *what*? God, I hate it when you do this stuff to me. If I'm so awful, why do you even bother—"

"Did I say I was finished? There's more. Jeez, you are so rude. So, we'll add rudeness. And you're ungrateful. You refuse to recognize any of the privileges that you enjoy. . . ."

I ran ahead of him now, down the middle of the abandoned tracks, trying to escape the litany of sins that I could still hear rolling out in a train-chug of a cadence. Finally, I just lay down across the tracks like a suicide.

"Yes, that's right," he said, approaching, not slowing, then stepping over me, "and you're a martyr."

I got up, charged after him, then tackled him to the best of my limited ability, dragging him down to the ground by his backpack like a lone hyena trying to take physically superior prey.

"This cannot possibly all be true," I said, more or less into the back of his head. "Or you wouldn't even be talking to me now."

He turned enough to give me the side of his face. He smelled like almond paste.

"Maybe it's because you remind me of a big iguana I once had. He whipped me in the face with his tail when all I was trying to do was share a piece of my exquisitely ripe mango with him."

"Hnnn," I said, remaining right next to his cheek to give his comparison theory the complete half-second consideration it deserved. "I don't think it would be worth all my million flaws just to be reminded of your violent, scaly, childhood pet that probably didn't even exist."

"He did exist, and I loved him. To be honest, I even kind of enjoyed the tail-slap. I tried to get him to do it again, but by then I think he was onto me."

"Right," I said in exasperation, shoving him down as I pushed off of him. I started down the tracks toward home again, and he scrambled up and ran alongside me again.

"You know the reason I put up with all that crap of yours, ya reptile?" he said. "It's because you are so funny."

"I'm not. Even I don't find me amusing."

"Well, that's that then, I'm out of explanations. Looks like all we're left with is, love is blind. Don't you hate being on the receiving end of a cliché?"

"What I hate is when I ask you to stop saying something and you continue saying it. Could you not say that again, please?"

He sighed loudly to produce a dramatic echo effect as we

crossed under the short trestle bridge just before his route home veered to the left.

"I'll try, Kiki," he said, splitting off and getting a safe few feet of distance away, "but I can't make any promises."

"No, you clearly cannot," I snapped. "Didn't I ask you—didn't I make you *promise* to stop that and call me by my given name?"

"That is your given name. I gave it to you," he said, walking backward down his road to give me just that bit of extra taunt. "You were almost gonna be Clyde Lovelette, until I came across Kiki Vandeweghe, which is certainly more you. You have the soul of a Kiki. I know you're in there. We need to save you from this sad-sack Kevin and release the Kiki within!"

"No," I said as he turned away and punched the air in some kind of freaky inexplicable triumph. "No, we don't."

He punched the air again then, with both fists, laughing. He so enjoyed himself, winding me up.

Jasper Jerk. Why would I miss a person like that? Why would I miss him even a little, never mind a lot?

OFF GRID

Maybe I came for more than the name.

My uncle Sydney lives in Crystal City. And he loathes my father. He told me several times that if I ever got it in my head to run away, I was welcome to come to him in Crystal City. Though I am not running away exactly—I am moving on and moving up—I think it's reasonable to assume the invitation still applies.

Sydney belongs to that long and dishonorable tradition in families called the black sheep. Every family really should have one and if they don't have a suitable candidate within the organization, then they should do a search, because I figure everyone needs their black-sheep services at least sometime in their lives.

My time is right now.

I don't give him any advance notice of my arrival because I have no contact details other than a street address. As far as I know, nobody else has such details either. He may or may not use phones and computers and other electronic devices but since he's been referred to more than once in our house as Off-the-Grid-Syd, it's kind of assumed that he doesn't.

I still carry with me like a pirate's tiny treasure map the directions to his house that he drew up and gave to me in a Batman card as a thirteenth-birthday present. "Doesn't look like much right now," he said with a wink, "but just you watch that sucker appreciate in value over the next few years."

He looks like a prophet today, as I stand on the little porch of the house at the address that I found in only three and a quarter hours and through the kindness of a half-dozen strangers. Two of whom turned out to be the wrong kind of kind and every kind of strange.

I press the doorbell three times before deciding it is broken or disabled, and then I knock.

I haven't even lowered my knocking hand before he throws the door open wide to me.

"Kevin!" he says, rushing out to give me a lung-busting hug.

"I hope you don't mind, Uncle Sydney," I gasp as he hugs out the last of my oxygen.

"Didn't I tell you? Huh? About that sucker appreciating in value? What are you now, seventeen?"

"Just last month," I say.

"And I missed it."

"That's okay."

"What's with the arm?" he asks, and I hold it up for him to examine as he tugs me inside. "And who wrote 'fuckwad' on it?"

"Your father. Did that?" Sydney asks, rather flabbergasted. He is referring to the injury beneath the cast, not Derek's defacement of it.

"My father. Yes."

He stares at me a few more seconds, working it out, doesn't get too far.

"*Your* father? When we were kids, flies used to pull *his* wings off."

"Listen, Sydney, we had a fight, all right? And I didn't get the better of it. I'd really just rather leave it at that, okay?"

"Okay," he says. "I have all I need to go on anyway. So, it's agreed, I'm going to kill your father for you."

"What? When did we agree to that? No, Syd, please, that's not the kind of thing I'd want at all."

"Really? Here, have another cookie."

"Thanks, and really."

"It wouldn't be any trouble. I've thought about killing that guy so many times over the years, the job would practically do itself. Pretty sure I have some plans drawn up somewhere."

"Well, no. I appreciate the gesture, though. Anyway, I'm fairly certain just my being here would kill him."

"Excellent point," he says, and points to make his point. "So, he knows you're here."

"Oh no, I just bolted, so he has no idea."

Uncle Sydney starts drumming his fingers loudly on the Formica table between us. He swivels a little side to side in his chair. His whole place is done up like a diner.

"You're not giving me much here, Nephew."

"Sorry, Sydney."

"Your father's not dead, he's not emotionally tormented by me, either . . ." He reaches across and snags the cookie package from in front of me. "And a whole pack of Pepperidge Farm Sausalitos. Is that all a whole pack of Pepperidge Farm Sausalitos buys a guy these days?"

He is having fun with me, but we both recognize the hot spots in his words just the same.

"He is emotionally tormented, Syd," I say weakly.

He sighs, nods. "Yeah, he is. But he always was."

I reach across and take the empty cookie pack back again, for no other reason than to seem less paralyzed than I feel.

"Can we not talk about him anymore?" I ask.

"Done," he says with an emphatic nod. Then we stare across at one another for several seconds before done comes undone. "Would be nice to ruin his career, at least. Can't be too many child-beating high-school headmasters out there in full employment."

"I'm not a child," I say.

He raises his hands in surrender. "Fair enough, Kevin. Still, I'd think he would be considered a danger to a school full of students."

"You know," I say, rising from the table as if I had someplace to go, "if I believed that, I would do something. But the truth is that the only two people he's a danger to are me and him."

"And his daughter and his wife, they don't count?"

There aren't enough Sausalitos in the world to make this hurt less.

"They don't count because they're gone, Syd. And because he never hurt them. Not physically."

He nods sadly. "Why didn't you stay with them, Kev? You should've gotten away clean and left him to rot away from the inside. What were you thinking?"

This is not a hard question to answer, in the sense that I know what I was thinking. On the other hand, it's very hard to answer, out loud, because most people—starting with the one I'm talking to—will never, ever get the logic of my dealings with Dad. Some days I have trouble piecing the logic back together myself, so I understand.

Dad didn't ever hurt the girls physically, this is true. But he hurt them.

The first of his midlife crises made a big mess of things. But it wasn't Armageddon.

The second, after he had slowly, incrementally, carefully been let back into the bosom of our family, was the one that brought the walls down.

Mum and Alice were wounded and enraged to the point where it is not conceivable that they will ever reconcile with Dad. It was faith betrayed, and to be forgiven once, to be given a do-over on that, would seem to be something that would make a man count himself blessed.

And so my father counted his blessings, and he took that do-over . . . and he did it over, again, a year later.

He left the house, the family, the town. He got a new job at a new school just far enough away. Everybody got a do-over.

Until I undid my do-over.

"I couldn't leave him by himself. I had to go back. He needed somebody. He needed me. He's a lot better than that, Syd, better than it seems on the outside, and somebody had to stick with him."

"Bullshit. He is what he is."

"He is a wonderful guy, a wonderful dad . . . almost all the time. I always thought I could help. And I always thought it was my job to do that. He needed me. I know nobody understood—"

"That's correct. I'm glad the girls got away from him anyway."

Glad. It's not a word that occurs often around the subject of Dad.

"Yeah," I say, failing to produce glad. "They saw red when I told them I was moving back with him. They were so livid, it was like when Mum threw him out, all over again. Screaming and breaking things, it got . . . fairly unpleasant. Things were said . . . some of them by me . . . It was bad. Is bad."

"Well, that I am sorry about. But, I am very glad you're here," he says, extra brightly for both of us. "I'm your whole family now."

"Thanks," I say. "That really does make me feel better. And it'll make me feel even more better if that's the end of that subject, okay?"

"Okay," he says, "done."

"Which way to the bathroom?"

He points, I start toward it, almost make it out of the room.

"Do your mother and sister know, Kevin? About the

latest? I bet they'd agree with me about your father's job situation."

I stop and spin back toward him.

"I wouldn't know, since I talk to them now about as often as I do you, and by the way, does the word 'done' have a different meaning here in Crystal City?"

He laughs. "I think you'll find that pretty much everything does, Nephew."

That sounds quite exciting to me at the moment.

"I'm going to look forward to that, Uncle."

"I like your style, boy."

"I'm glad. And right now, my style says 'done' means 'done.'"

"Done."

I run to the bathroom before "done" can try to mean anything else.

Uncle Sydney's house is very small, and the second bedroom is his office. But it's a nice little spot with a window overlooking a dusty Little League baseball field, a chain-link cage of an asphalt tennis/basketball court beyond it, and a section of slow narrow waterway beyond that. The couch, being covered in some kind of vinyl leatherette material like practically everything else in the place, needs a lot of sheet, pillow, and blanket help to achieve true comfortability, but we do eventually get it there.

And once I lay my head down, I crash, plummeting through all layers of consciousness and unconsciousness to the point where my uncle's knocking on my forehead like a door thirteen hours later still sounds like he's eight feet away and rapping on the actual door.

"Wow," I say, lying flat and staring up at him as he continues knocking just for kicks.

"Yeah, wow. Guess you needed a little nap there."

"It was great. Could you stop the knocking now?"

"Sure," he says, straightening up and walking away. "Meet me in the kitchen, breakfast is ready."

"Oh, that's really thoughtful, but I usually don't eat till—"

"Most important meal of the day, Kev. So get your ass out here, unless you want to look like that for the rest of your life."

He shuts the door behind him with a pop.

Thanks for that, Syd. I must be clashing with his décor.

The breakfast that awaits me is a steak so big it has to have been made from more than one cow. It's covered in sautéed onions and mushrooms and sitting on a bed of raw spinach, with an honor guard of bright red plum tomatoes all around the periphery. Just breathing the air of this kitchen makes me satisfied and stronger.

"Well, you're not gonna get the color back in your face just by looking at it, Kevin. Sit, boy, eat."

"This *is* a color," I say, pointing at my face, "and it is *my* color." I sit.

"Yeah, well there *is* a cure for it, and *this* is it," he says, taking a seat across from me with an identical plate of abundance. "And never mind the color, what's with the texture? Looks like you had skin grafts or something."

"Jesus, you're a kind uncle. I had some acne a while back, okay? Doctor said stress probably had a lot to do with it."

"I don't doubt it. But what did he treat it with, paint stripper?"

I feel like the muscles at the back of my neck have just given up entirely. My head falls forward. I am staring at the edge of the table right in front of me, and I have no desire to ever look anywhere else again.

How is a guy supposed to outrun everything, including his own face?

Next thing I sense is that my stealthy uncle—he is quiet like a cat burglar when he wants to be—has come around the table, circled behind me, and has his cheek pressed alongside my cheek.

"I'm sorry, Kevin. I was just playing with you. I never had any kids or zits. So I'm kind of an oaf with some things. I'll get better."

His kindness helps, and I feel like raising my head. But I don't, not until he pulls away from me and I am left with the sensation on my skin, the scent in my nostrils.

My dad. Every element of that moment for me was crawling with his brother, my father, right down to the opening "I'm sorry, Kevin," which prefaced so many repairs, so many recoveries.

He retakes his seat across from me, points his steak knife at my steak, and I think I get his point.

I start eating, though I cannot envision ever finishing.

"What I should have said," he says, "is that I never had a kid, until now."

I have to smile at his gesture, a cube of beef suspended on the tines of the fork in front of my lips.

"That's a damn nice thing to say."

"Well, I damn mean it, dammit."

"Okay, but this is only temporary until I get myself oriented. I will not be bothering you for long."

"Well, there ya go, I was just about to tell you the exact same thing." He laughs heartily, though we both understand that he means every syllable, as I believe he means every syllable of everything he says. Chowing down is how we seal the deal.

I make the appropriate moans of approval as I chew—as much as I even need to—the first buttery bite of beef. "Fantastic, Uncle Sydney, no kidding."

"That pleases me greatly," he says.

"There's no way I could eat all this food, though."

He is chewing, so he holds up a hold-on finger till he's ready. Then, he's ready.

"There is a way. And you will find it."

"But it's massive."

"There's a big T-bone in there somewhere, so it's really not as much meat as it looks like. In this place, we get our protein, our fresh fruit and vegetables to the tune of at least eight portions a day, seeds, nuts, whole grains, plenty of hydration. Gimme a few days and I'll turn you into the man somebody else couldn't manage in seventeen years. Not certain how much I can do for that complexion, but we'll start by cutting out sugar and see where we go from there."

Since nothing in there seemed like an invitation to debate, I don't debate with him. I still don't think if we managed to clone me, twice, all of my selves could finish, but this one is going to give it a try.

My uncle is a methodical eater. It could well be that he is putting on a how-to-eat clinic for my benefit, but the way he fully interacts with each item and each mouthful makes me think he's a natural. The result is that there is a calm, welcome quiet to the meal while he focuses, and a jarring breaking of that calm after he neatly wipes his mouth with his napkin.

"I'll be away for a few days on business," he says while

pretending not to stare at my slow-moving knife and fork.

"Okay," I say.

My father always said that his brother was a filthy criminal. I can see for myself he has the fussy cleanliness of a cat, so that's one myth busted. Also, my father's unique take on truth was, "A statement containing an inaccurate detail or two is not a lie if it is serving a larger, more honest narrative." So, you could say his pronouncements about his brother or anybody else's were not necessarily take-it-to-the-bank reliable.

"Can I ask you a question, Uncle Sydney?"

"You want to know what it is I do."

I nod.

"You know, Kevin, I'm happy to tell you anything. But, sometimes just knowing things is enough to get you into trouble or play havoc with your inner peace. Maybe safe and simple is the better way to go with your life."

I look at him for a long minute while he does the same to me, a something across his mouth that could be a smile but is not quite declaring itself. I don't think I've ever met anyone quite as sure as he is, and I have to say I find that extremely powerful and alluring.

"Are you telling me that you recommend 'safe and simple' as a rule for life, Uncle?"

His smile declares itself fully now and he reacts as if I have flipped over the right card.

"I am categorically not telling you that, Nephew."

Who could resist?

"I would love to know what it is you do."

"I am a large-scale transporter, basically, of luxury goods. Mostly fine cars, but whatever high-margin items come available. I see to it that these items find their way far, far away from their stinking-rich former legal owners, to distant places where their new, somewhat less well-off owners can enjoy them without suffering undue anxiety over it. It is perfectly reasonable redistribution of wealth in my opinion and a victimless crime. Like necrophilia."

"I can see what—whoa, the last part there just caught up to me."

"Ah, don't worry about it. That's just a thing I say. And until somebody with dough comes along and offers me good money to do some necro-pimping, that is not a part of my portfolio."

"Oh," I say, still kind of stumbling over it all. "Yeah. Sure. Right."

"So then, there. I have given you my full confidence and trust. Feel good?"

I am shocked—on several levels, actually. But shocked, really, at how good that does make me feel. I'm bigger than I was a minute ago. Could be the steak, I suppose. Steak and confidence, more like it.

"I feel good," I say.

"And are we good, with the reality and all? I don't need to worry about you knowin'?"

"Not at all, Syd. No worries, and we are good."

"Good. So, the house is all yours, three, maybe four days. I take off later this afternoon. Rules. Keep it clean, just like you see it now."

It glistens. "Yes, sir."

"Stay outta my room. Even if it's on fire."

"Understood."

"And the place is all yours, but *only* yours. No guests, no exceptions. If you get lucky, go out and use the baseball field like everybody else."

"That would not be a problem, Uncle Sydney. Much as I wish it would be."

"Sheesh. Is that why you were inquiring about sex with dead people?"

"I never in—"

"With confidence like that, it's no wonder you can't bag a live specimen. Eat your steak, practice your swagger, and when I come back I want to see some rotten punk attitude."

He makes me laugh, at myself, and it somehow doesn't even hurt.

"I'll see what I can do," I say. "But here, first can you sign my cast before you go?"

"It would be an honor." I offer him my stubby marker and he snorts, before walking past me. "Gimme a break with that thing. I got about a thousand Montblancs in the office."

He comes back and signs with a flourish. Once we finish eating we take our plates together out to the kitchen where we each wash our own stuff. Then he guides me around, showing me what I need to know about the washer-dryer, what's available to me in the freezer and what's not, and vitally, his vast armory of cleaning products and accessories underneath the sink and the garbage disposal. We move on to the hallway, the linen cupboard, the bathroom, the towels and toiletries, and eventually every last item in the house that has a button, switch, plug, or any remote possibility of a dopey rookie like me creating havoc.

"How are you for dough?" he asks me, all serious as he fishes a single key on a moose-head key chain out of the small single-drawer table under the coat hooks by the front door.

"I'm good," I say. "I'm okay for now."

"But you'll let me know," he says, opening the door to the street and ushering me out ahead of him.

"I'm hoping I won't have to," I say, "but yeah, it's huge, knowing you're there covering my ass like that. Thanks a whole lot, Sydney. But right, when you're not here . . ."

No idea why I expected a guy like Syd to step in and

finish a sentence I could not finish for myself. His raised eyebrow would have to do.

"If you're away on business, and it turns out I have to contact you in an emergency because I *am* short of dough or whatever, and my ass *does* need covering . . . well, how will I reach you?"

I know that I'm stretching a bit. That I'm looking for a key to a special exclusive club that I may never need, but jeezuz I want that key all the same just to be special and exclusive.

"You won't," he says with a friendly dangerous uncle smile. "You'll reach around behind you and cover your own ass until I return. Got it?"

"Got it."

Uncle Sydney claps a hand on my shoulder as we head off on our circuit of the neighborhood. He shows me where to get essentials that might not already be in the house, which would be none. He shows me the shoe repair shop, which I will never need in my whole life, but when we go inside and I meet Carlo and smell the leather and shake the old rocky hand, I feel like there was something beyond shoes in the visit and come out glad I had the honor. We visit three small eating establishments, each one smelling different, of lamb and baked goods, of simmering tomatoes and spring onions and basil and cinnamon and peaches, and none of which has a deep-fat fryer.

Conspicuously, Syd and I stay by the entrance all three times. We breathe it in, the busy folks behind the counter notice us and wave, and Syd points at me before we exit again.

"You'll be well taken care of, any of these places. You'll never go hungry."

"I'm not hungry now, but I want to eat in all of them anyway."

"Ha," he says, "that's the stuff. You'll be great here. That's the municipal pool right there, and the public library . . . it's a great neighborhood. Never have to leave it if you don't want to."

"I want to, though," I say, not meaning any disrespect to the fullness of Syd's neighborhood universe.

He laughs again. "Of course you do, young man. You're a young man. You want to go explore. So go, explore. I'll probably be gone by the time you get back. You know what to do," he says, pointing at me so close I can smell the soap on his finger.

"I do know what to do," I say.

"And you know what to not do," he says.

"I do."

He gives me a hug and surprises me by holding it a fair bit of time, and firmly.

"Are you sure you don't need some money?" he asks while his DNA once again passes my smell test.

"You must be joking," I say as we part and I back away from him down the road. "I feel like I owe you so much already."

He stands steady, seeing me off with a big windshield-wiper wave.

"I sort of feel like I owe you more, 'cause of him," he says.

JASPER JUDGE

So who told you to go sneaking around the dark corners of his computer anyway? That's insane, and guaranteed to produce nothing but horrors. *Nobody* could pass that test. I'm telling you, nobody."

Jasper apparently didn't think it was smart of me to snoop on my father's computer. He very nearly snapped the tops off of six of my fingers when he threw himself at the laptop and banged it shut.

Truth be told, it was a relief.

"I guess now we know why he didn't want me to move back in with him," I said.

"So, he has a life," Jasper said. "He's entitled to that, isn't he? Are you still four or something, expecting his world to cease whenever he's not with you? If that's it, then he'd be right to not want you for a roommate. I wouldn't."

"You call *that* a life?" I shouted, jumping up out of my father's private desk chair behind his private desk in his until-recently-private home, and pointing with my fist at that private computer and the shocks within it that I had no business looking at.

It probably would have been a good idea to let him know when I was coming. I didn't, because it never for a second occurred to me that he would have been anything less than totally thrilled at my returning to him. That possibility never crossed my mind.

He was less than totally thrilled.

"I do," Jasper said, mostly calmly. "I call it a life. It might not be *my* version of life—or it might be—and it's surely not *your* version of life, but it is definitely some people's version, and without a doubt it's his right to have it. Frankly, it's not even that weird."

"Of course it is."

"You are very, very naive, Kiki my friend."

"I am not. Not naive, and not Kiki. And not wrong."

I didn't really know whether I was or wasn't any of those things. Because all I knew then was that I was hurt and that I needed to get over it or through it or under it or whatever a person was supposed to do with this kind of ache, but I was getting nowhere with it. Nowhere.

It hurt a lot, feeling like I didn't belong in Dad's house, his life, his home.

"Well, I suppose you could always virus his computer," Jasper said, leaning over the back of me in the desk chair and reopening the laptop. He clicked back rapidly to the most appalling, *not* enthralling smut site of the many on my father's favorites. Then he made a low *ow-yeow* sound of both injury and satisfaction right in my ear that made the whole thing infinitely ickier.

My turn to slam it closed. *Slam*.

"A virus?" I said, jumping up out of the chair quickly enough to bang Jasper's chin with my shoulder. "Sorry," I said, "but, I hardly think a virus is going to do much since I'm sure everyone at *that* party has already contracted every disease known to man. They are probably now a filthy invincible master race of degenerate—"

"No, *The Master Race* was the name of the video before that one, where it was just those five naked guys in director's chairs facing the—"

"I remember the race, thank you."

I led him out of my father's study and to the living room where I was determined to find the most normal and sensation-free programming on TV to numb the next hour or so.

"You know that's not the kind of virus I meant, right?" he said as we sat on the couch, searching.

I turned to stare at him while I continued to blindly click through the stations. "Yes. I was making a joke."

"Oh. Sorry, I just never heard you do that before. I mean, you're funny all over the place, but not usually with that kind of, you know, intention. That was good, though."

"Thanks," I said, still locking onto him as if somewhere in his eyes I might find answers to the questions I couldn't even formulate yet. I stopped clicking and settled on the voice of somebody excitable selling us something fabulous involving juices. "Are you comfortable?" was the concoction that came out of me.

Jasper's expression went from amused to confused to concerned over several seconds. He inched a bit away from me, but it was more like he was trying to get me in focus than a prelude to fleeing.

"Well," he said, "it appears Daddy's Pornotopia had a bigger effect on you than you thought."

"No, no, what I mean is . . . oh God, don't *call* it that."

Strange as it may have sounded, Jasper and I were actually kind of perfect as friends. I watched him there, practically tumbling off the couch laughing at my reaction, my squawk of outrage, my feathers flying all over the room, and I could not help converting to his way of thinking. I laughed at myself, which I knew was far too rare an occurrence. My anxiety lessened, a little bit, for a moment.

He made me get over myself, however briefly. And I liked it there, over myself.

"What I am asking, Jasper, is what do you think of this place? Do you like my father's house? Is it homey?"

He scanned all around, serious and intense, which I knew meant he was nothing of the kind. Then he turned to me again, fixed me with spooky, unfocused eyes, and spoke in a sickly singsong voice. "This is a lovely home you have here. Lovely home. Lovely home. It just needs a juicer. You need a juicer, Kiki. Kiki, buy the juicer now."

I looked toward the TV, where the screechy and jittery info-pitchman was going on rabidly about the life-changing capabilities of the juicer.

"Well done," I said. "But, really."

"Really, um, no offense, but there's not really anything for me to go on. It's an all right place. Kinda bland. Not a lot of personality, warmth. But it's okay, I guess. Comfortable enough."

I looked at him silently for a few ticks, and I nodded.

"I think the house makes me angry," I said.

Once more Jasper gave me the quizzical expression.

"So, you want me to go have a word with my house, have it come over here and kick your house's ass?"

"Yeah," I snapped, "would you, please, and then we can watch them fight? Just shut up for a second, will you? I think

I know what I'm trying to say, and I need to say it before that window closes."

With that, Jasper pulled a shocking maneuver on a par with my attempting to construct a joke—he got earnest and respectful.

"Go," he said, hammer-punching my knee like a judge's gaveling.

"I was so sure this was where I belonged. I was *so sure* this was the right decision that I pretty well destroyed the remaining other part of my life to be here. Now I'm here, and Dad seems just confused by my presence. And this house, right, it's not somebody's home. Certainly not my home. And not his, either, in any real way. If I just broke in like a burglar I would not have a clue I was robbing my own father. He has no pictures, no . . . I don't know, stupid knickknacks, mementos from those years, you know. It's cold and it's blank, and I hate it and it's this way by *design*, I realize, because he is trying to forget it all. He's wiping it, making like our previous life never was."

He was holding his composure an impressive length of time, and I appreciated the hell out of it.

"It was a wicked divorce, you said," he said.

I nodded, nodded, nodded.

"And I understand all that," I said. "I really do. But, I'm *here* now, Jas. I'm fucking *right here*!" I was shouting, and aware, and did not care. "I am the solution to that problem, aren't I? And now, look, I'm going to cry and I *fucking hate* that, too."

"That's cool," he said. "Afterward you'll feel better. You'll be able to relax some."

"I don't want to relax. This is exactly the way I'm supposed to feel. I'm doing just what I'm supposed to and he is not, goddammit."

"Am I stupid if I say maybe you should talk to him about this?"

"Yes, you are, but it's not your fault. It's him. Of course I talked to him. But I can't talk to him, not about something he doesn't want to let out. I never could. He's good with words, you see."

"You're good with words. You're great with words."

I shook my head vigorously enough that I felt as if I could sense my brain sloshing against the insides of my skull. "No, he is of a different order. The only thing that ever drove me on to get better with language was to catch up with him, to meet him *there.* But *there* was always elsewhere by the time I got there. He would always leave me in a state of thinking we had talked about what I wanted to talk about but only later would I realize that the real things, the stuff he wasn't offering up, didn't come away with me at all the way I thought it did. The only difference now, since

I have been here, is that I know this is how it goes. So when he starts it, when I see it happening, I don't play on. I rage, Jasper. I pop off and I know I sound like I am criminally insane. I know it, but cannot do anything about it. It's the fact that this time he is doing the puffs of smoke, the hymns in praise of his own evanescence, for the purpose of making me disappear."

He got up off the couch and walked toward me, and I only then realized I had walked and ranted, paced and panted, until I had taken up a kind of defense position in front of the TV screen.

"No," I shouted at him. "Stay there, I mean it." I believed they were fists I had created there at the far ends of my arms as Jasper advanced, breached my defenses, and gave me what I could only guess was a mighty fatherly hug.

"It was *his* fucking Robert Frost," I said into Jasper's shoulder.

"Okay, pal," he said patting my back with increasing firmness, which must have been the technique for bucking a guy up. "I don't need to understand every damn thing you say in order to be supportive."

"*Home is the place where, when you have to go there/ they have to take you in*. Robert Frost. He gave me that, goddammit. He planted it right inside my skull, and right inside my rib cage. He knows."

"Though, in fairness," Jasper said tentatively, "he did take you in."

"Like hell he did," I growled, and simultaneously felt him go stiff and then loosen his grip.

I turned just in time to see my father evanesce, out of the doorway, up the stairs.

GOOD IDEA

My uncle's no-guests rule strikes me as a pretty decent cruel-funny joke since at this very moment the only active member of my invite-a-pal-over list would be him.

So it's natural enough that I am headlong on the path to rectifying the friendlessness situation. I feel the strangeness of the key in my pocket, withdraw it, then pause staring at the dangling brass beauty hanging off the end of the moose-head key chain. This constitutes one of the simple pleasures I plan to enjoy in the new life I'm composing for myself. It had been six months since I had had my own key, to let myself in if I was curfew transgressive. Not only do I not now ever have to sleep on the porch, I can come home to my own, empty place. Mine.

As I stride the street I have a shiny black Montblanc in

one pocket, a key in another, and something of a waddle to my walk because dammit, I ate every last bit of Syd's beautiful beast breakfast and it feels like it will be with me for some time. Because Kiki Vandeweghe doesn't skip the most important meal of the most important day.

Crystal City indeed.

I passed through a good bit of the city when I bumbled around trying to find Syd's place, but I couldn't really say I saw it. As I retrace much of it now it begins opening itself more fully and I begin entering it for real.

It's not quite as polished as the name might imply. There are lots of shiny parts, that's for sure, with some blocks being completely unbroken strings of neon-and-video shopfront windows. I like the fact that some parts of the commercial zones are a complete jumble of different businesses like cheap electronics next to a tarot reader next to a shoe shop next to a holistic medicine and massage therapy shop. I like the fact that that district is followed immediately by another block that is all about motors—used cars, car repairs, car parts, motorcycles, and biker gear.

I like the fact that the city is large enough to even have zones. Ass Bucket was just one zone.

When I feel I've picked up enough of the city's bars and restaurants and gyms and playgrounds full of guys like me just sprung loose for the summer, I catch a whiff of the river not far off. I follow my nose until I reach it. It's a canal, actually, and I walk along the towpath between the water and the hip-high dry grass for a while. I feel like a big cat, all stealth and stalking, as I walk into the sun and toward the bus station.

It is the only idea I have, other than to walk aimlessly and endlessly for the rest of my life until I find her again. And if I don't find her, it will be the end of my life even if that's tomorrow. Because then I'd just start yet another new life and hope it works out better.

I figure there's no limit to the number of times you can reboot if you need to. Unless there is a limit. Let's hope I never have to find out.

As I approach the line of glass doors at the front of the bus station, I suffer a small flutter of worry that had not troubled me at all as I'd marched my way through *my* new city, all new, clean slate, yet to be written. Suddenly, as I see my reflection there, I see the uncertainty, and the need. I see the chump who was not supposed to follow me onto that bus. The reality is that you can be anybody you want to, as long as you don't have to see yourself.

I shove the door out of the way as I muscle myself into the station like a real man on a real man's mission.

"Hey, jackass," she snaps as she catches the door with her good hand.

"Sorry, sorry, sorry," I say, nothing at all like a real man on a mission but everything like a little boy on his knees. Then, "Hey! Stacey!" I shout, again letting honest emotion obliterate my cool. Got to stop that.

"Did you try and bash me with that door on purpose?"

"No, of course not."

"Well, you were staring right at me when you did it."

"Staring right at . . . ? No, no, it was my reflection. In the glass. It's very bright out here. Completely unintentional I assure you."

"Okay, good. 'Cause the door assault was bad enough, but that foul look you were giving to whoever it was, that was true murder."

"Yeah, well, I am a killer after all."

"Um, uh-huh, sure. So, killer, what happened yesterday? With Mr. Derek? We were motoring so fast, by the time we stopped for a breath he was nowhere to be seen and neither were you."

"Oh, that. I kicked his ass."

"Phwaaaaa-ha . . ."

She laughs for long enough that I look at my watch. Then I join in, but at roughly 10 percent of her gusto.

"Sorry," I say, "did I say 'kicked'? I meant 'tripped.'"

"Ha. Really? Did you get him?"

"Right onto his face. Broke his cast in half too."

"Way to go, you. The Cast Avenger!" She extends her cast-fist and bumps with mine.

Then, emerging out of nowhere or possibly Stacey's backpack, is Molly. She sticks her cast into the celebration. "What's this for?" she asks.

"Hi, Molly," I say.

"We're paying proper respect to the boy who saved the day yesterday," Stacey says. "Word's all over town how he gave that Derek character a good public flogging, defending *your* virtue."

"*Real*-ly?" she gasps and looks up at me with a big dewy-gooey-eyed expression that nobody has ever looked at me with before. It's a little bit thrilling and frightening.

"It was kind of less swashbuckling than that," I say.

"And modest, too," Stacey says, elbowing Molly, making a show of making mischief. "By the way, I looked you up, Mr. Vandeweghe, and you're holding up pretty well for a guy who played in the NBA thirty years ago. You never played any defense, apparently, so maybe that kept your mileage down."

Ah, for God's sake, here comes the blushing. I can feel my head just about percolating.

"It's a common name," I say.

"Right. Anyway, Kiki, so what are you doing back here? One night on the street enough to convince you to go home where you belong?"

"I am not a street person. I came here to see somebody."

"Right, so did I. I just don't know who it is yet. So then, what are you doing back at the lovely bus palace?"

Think, think, think. Be cool, don't be pathetic and needy.

"I didn't come looking for you, if that's what you're thinking."

"That is what I'm thinking," she says boldly, grinning right in my face and probably having the time of her life.

"It's a little bit sad, then," Molly says, sadly. "Because we came looking for you."

"Yes, sir, we did," Stacey says, firm and proud.

Why can't I be firm and proud and just say what I mean and live with that meaning without coming off as some kind of a gink?

"Come on, Molly," she adds, towing her past me and out the door I just came in through. "Looks like we've been dumped."

"Dummy," I say, banging my cast sharply off my temple. Twice.

I rush back out through that door, taking a right turn this time, and quick-step up the street after them.

"There are laws against what you're doing to us here, KV," Stacey calls out, embarrassingly loud. She doesn't bother looking back at me even though most everyone else on the busy sidewalk does, including a smiling and waving Molly.

"Where are we going?" I ask.

"Are we a 'we' now?" Stacey asks.

"Ah, let's be a 'we,'" Molly says.

"I'd like that," I say. "Yes." Then I remember my two years of French, and because I am such a smoothie decide to put it to use. "*Oui*. See, I just agreed in French there, see? *Oui* and we? So how can you resist?"

"With moves like that, why would we even want to?"

I'm rolling now.

Where we wind up is a place known as Crystal Beach, which is actually the short stretch of gritty, sandy, marshy land along which the city's working waterfront is joined by the canal. It's not the kind of recreational beach you would go to if you had a *beach* to go to, but it has what you might call charms of its own. There is trash here and there on the ground, and a faint taste of iron in the salty air. You'd have to be of a certain *stripe* to see this as a destination shore.

Such as a bunch of kids roughly our age gathering in groups and gaggles, kicking balls around, chucking rocks and each other into the water, and generally treating Crystal Beach like it is not only a proper beach but also its own population within a population.

If a particularly hard-core high school had, among its facilities, its own waterfront, it would look a lot like Crystal Beach.

And the reason we are now a part of it is that we have as our guide somebody in the know.

"So, are you actually *from* here, Molly?" Stacey asks, plunking down cross-legged in the sand, facing the water and the commercial boats chugging across the bay. Molly and I sit on either side of her in a sea-facing crescent formation.

"What?" Molly says, waving the idea away like it's an unusually comical mosquito. "Oh gosh, nobody is from Crystal City as far as I know."

"But, it's your home now," I say.

She looks my way, seems about to answer, then gives me both a shrug and a nod. "My mother and me. This is where we came to."

She stops right there, and appears to think that's enough.

"So, you live with your mother," I say.

"Nope. She hated the place, didn't last a day here. Mother was never very patient. The whole of Crystal City smells exactly like my father did, apparently. He worked on fishing boats. Mother said she had already vomited away enough of her days because of that man and she wasn't going through that hee-haw ever again. Right back on the bus she went."

"How come you didn't go with her?"

Molly looks over to Stacey as if I'm joking or something, then back to me. "Because it's great here, obviously," she says. "'Suit yourself, kiddo,' is what Mother told me to do and so

I suited myself. I think she's suiting herself too, but I'm not sure."

Stacey leans over and pulls Molly into a quick neck hug, then releases her again.

"She stays in a Catholic hostel here in town," Stacey says. "I stayed there last night myself. Not bad. Comfortable, but you gotta deal with the church-every-morning business, which—"

"I thought you said you liked church," Molly says.

"I said I liked churches that had bedrooms attached."

"Can just anybody stay there, for free?" I ask.

"Only if there's room," Molly says, "and if a resident sponsors you."

"I'm a friend of Molly, Molly's a friend of Jesus, and so I'm all tucked in and comfy. Sorry, Kiki, no room at the inn for you."

"You can come," Molly says anxiously. "We'll find some room." She's up on her haunches and leaning toward me, saucer-eyed. She has a look that makes you want to make things better for her.

"I'm okay, thanks," I say. "I have a place. A relative in the city. He even made me an incredible breakfast, massive steak, and onions, and—"

"That's what I smelled," Stacey says, leaning close to me. "Oh, man oh man, you sure landed on your feet."

"True enough. I never saw steaks like this. Hardly even had to chew, and with the salad and the mushrooms and onions all sautéed—"

"Shush," Molly says, looking at the variety of beach bums all around.

"Huh? Why?"

"Because that's the kind of breakfast some people would kill you for. And some others would kill you just for *talking* about."

Stacey starts laughing, then realizes she's the only one and starts laughing even harder.

"Okay, calm down you two," she says. "The chances of anybody killing you are not that great. But the chances of them following your onion-scented ass back to the *source* of such riches might be pretty good."

"Yes," Molly concurs. "Everybody steals. Everybody, everybody. But especially that bunch over there." She points to a half-dozen people who are draped all over a cluster of boulders half in and half out of the water. They are mostly motionless, slapped onto the rocks like big starfish, and they are all so skinny it's hard to tell what the male-female breakdown is. "When they aren't here, they're either out trying to steal stuff or they're pacing back and forth in front of the pharmacy waiting for it to open so they can get their methadone."

"Wait, I think I passed by that pharmacy," I say, as if she's just mentioned a treasured old landmark.

"It's between the closed-down movie theater and the sex-shop-dry-cleaners."

"That's it."

"Yeah, every decent-size town's got them guys," Stacey says. "The Green Party."

"Yes!" Molly says.

Stacey reads the small confusion on my face and helps me out. "It's because they're kinda green, if you get up close. Don't get up close."

"Right," I say. "I get it. Don't get too close to the Greens, and don't give anybody the bright idea to rob me."

"You're welcome," she says brightly. "Now, let's go to your place and party."

Aw, hell.

"Oh," I say, getting up and stretching. I am only lately realizing that when I hit a tense part of conversation I spring into preflight mode. "It's . . . not like that. Maybe at some point. But right now I'm not in a position to have full rights to the place to that extent. Possibly after a while, when my uncle gets to see that—"

I interrupt my own explanation to address the disruption that has broken out among my audience. Stacey is sniggering, covering her mouth with her hand and leaning over Molly heavily enough to topple her. Molly, for her part, looks stunned.

"Did I say something funny?" I ask. I hear in my voice that my next line should be "Would you care to share the joke with the rest of the class?" But it's already too late to help it.

"Oh, come on, Kiki. That kinda booty-breakfast doesn't come from nobody's *uncle*. Unless, well, right, unless it's *that* kind of uncle, in which case hey, fair dues to you, dude, for doing what you got to do."

"Hey!" I say.

She waits, still leaning on top of Molly.

But I've got nothing more compelling than "He is my uncle."

"Isn't he just adorable," Molly says.

"He so is," Stacey says.

"I am *not* adorable," I shout, managing to bring more unwanted attention my way. A guy who's dressed like Robinson Crusoe turns and smiles broadly at me. Then he whips a Frisbee from about ten yards away. I see it all the way and it still sails through my hands and hits me in the throat.

"That's assault, Mickey," Molly says as the guy comes to retrieve his disk.

He leans uncomfortably close and says, "That was not assault. But you're right, man, you're not adorable." He runs off and rejoins his game with the debatably more beautiful people.

"Don't listen to him," Molly says.

"Did he hurt your feelings?" Stacey asks with something less than full feeling.

"I think I'll recover," I say. "What *is* this place anyway?" I ask, scanning the landscape, which I suddenly and uncharitably think of as land-scrape.

"It's The Beach," Molly chirps.

"Not like any beach I've ever come across," I say.

"I'm sure it's not," Stacey says. "I've only been here a couple times before, the only other time I came to Crystal City. True enough, it's not what a lot of folks would be looking for in a beach. But it's cool. Pretty open with characters. Mostly safe."

"Mostly," I echo.

"Well, sure. No place is totally safe. Ain't that right, Miss Molly?"

Molly looks fleetingly at Stacey and then whips her head away toward the bay. Down at the waterline, a pack of three big mutty dogs emerges from by the canal and starts splashing around, yipping and pawing at each other. Molly coos, squeals, and tears off toward them like she's their long lost fourth member.

Stacey and I watch her, like parents. Feral though they

seem to be, the dogs take her in and include her as if they had been expecting her all along.

"So, you guys are pals, now," I say.

"I guess. 'Pals' is a kinda stupid word though."

You have to figure you can't offend anybody with the word "pals." I look to the side and watch Stacey watching Molly with grim intensity.

"You're probably good for her."

"I probably am. Just by virtue of not having a dick, I think I'm good for her."

First, I'm shocked into silence. Then, I'm shocked into looking away from her toward Molly and her canine pack.

"I'm sorry," I say. "I'll be quiet."

My magical mystical powers of amusement have somehow worked on Stacey again, because she leans forward with her head on her knees and her mouth open in a silent laugh. Then she straightens up and slaps me on the leg.

"Didn't mean you, Kiki. Your dick isn't a problem for anybody."

Ah, come on, now.

You wait an entire lifetime for a girl like Stacey to even contemplate . . . *that* . . . and then it finally happens. It was not what I had hoped it would be.

"I'm outta here," I snap, jumping to my feet like the big sand-mottled jerk-in-the-box that I feel like.

I pass right across her line of vision and am almost away when she catches me midstomp, midhuff, by the ankle and brings me right down to the ground once more.

I am lying in the sand, facing away from her, feeling the strong grip on my ankle and lost for any next moves.

"Don't make me drag you," she says.

The triple play of humiliation would have been too much to bear so I twist and scoot myself back to sit next to her again.

I stare stone-faced at Molly as she marches back up to the beach toward us.

"I promise I didn't mean any disrespect to you," Stacey says, then leans close to my ear, "or your dick. I'm sure it's a wonderful thing for what it is."

I hear my asthma breath whistling in, and my blushing face is so hot and fluidy, I am surely going to start oozing tears of blood. God, I am a mess.

Then, just before Molly arrives, Stacey kisses me softly, just at the smooth spot right in front of my ear.

"I *knew* this was a good idea," I say, yup, right out loud.

INSIDE OUT

After Dad and Mom split up for good, we all shot off like meteorites in different directions. Everybody got angry all of a sudden. Okay, maybe not Alice, but that was only because she was already angry. Mom and Dad were both always saying it was just a phase when she shouted three or four times a day that she hated somebody or everybody. Then, when things got toxic between the parents, it was sort of like that YOU BROKE IT, YOU BOUGHT IT sign at the Precious Pieces gift shop because Angry Alice became Always Angry Alice.

During that time I decided to read every piece of literature that had people our age and that contained any form of the word "outsider" in the title or synopsis.

I gave up after two months because it turned out that by

the time I read every book that fit that description I wouldn't even remember ever being this age.

And also, every outsider I read about had a life that I envied so badly it made me depressed to think about it.

I just had to be someplace else. I had always felt like this to some degree. Just right over there, or there, or just beyond, was certainly the place that was waiting to welcome me. I never, all through school, made any strong attachments to people before I met Jasper, which was what gave me this outsider-outside-the-outsiders feeling.

Unless it was the other way around.

"Oh, it was you, no doubt about it," Jasper said practically before I could finish the question. I was talking while paddling—playing table tennis in Dad's garage. But as soon as the ball returned to me I belted it, over Jasper's head and loudly off the metal garage door. He calmly walked over to the door behind him, bent, and picked up the badly dented ball. "Was this necessary?" he asked, holding the ball out for me to see.

"So it's all my own fault, never fitting in?" I asked as I leaned with both hands flat on the table.

"Yes," he said, mirroring me from his side. "I think maybe you get off on the rejection, outsider, victim thing. You seem to like being wounded and offended."

"Stop judging me. I hate being judged."

Then he just started being dramatic. He allowed himself to flop forward, his forehead on the table and his arms spread wide. Didn't stop him talking crap, however.

"You ask either/or questions, knowing that one of the answers will make you outraged. You move to a new school/home/town in April. Of junior year. Without announcing yourself or even making a basic scouting trip in advance. If you marched up and down every street in town wearing a sandwich sign that said 'Ostracize Me Now!' on one side and 'Oh by the way, go fuck yourselves!' on the other, you would have arrived at the same friendlessness without having to wonder about the whole, 'Gee, is it me?' question."

Continuing to be dramatic for whatever reason, Jasper remained facedown on the table.

"I'm not friendless," I said more gently than I had intended to. "I have you to prevent that. And you have me, so we're square."

He raised just his head and faced me so he looked like a smiling airplane lying on the green runway of the Ping-Pong table. "You're square, I'm . . . I don't know, rhomboid or something. I have plenty of friends. I just don't show them to you because you'll scare them away. Then I'll be like you. Which would be tragic."

I was about to attempt to defend myself when the electric garage door startled me with its loud rumbling opening.

"It's my dad," I said nervously, like I'd been caught breaking in or something.

"Oh, good timing, naughty principal," Jasper said, holding his compromised position.

"That is *not* funny," I barked, making him cackle helplessly as he unfolded himself and we frantically folded up the table so my father could have his garage back.

After I had my freak-out and told Jasper how I felt about my dad and me, about being homeless within my father's house, he spent a generous amount of his valuable wind-me-up time on winding me down again. He convinced me to give it time, to let Dad think things through, to let us evolve again as some kind of unit, and then maybe I would eventually hear the kinds of words I was hoping to hear when I first came.

Hope, then, was my plan of action. Hope, the chump's choice for when you've got nothing else.

Perhaps that was the kind of doomsaying I'd need to leave behind. It wouldn't be easy.

Of course my father had a life and a right to have it. I never should have gone looking around like I did on his computer. It was wrong.

Wrong, wrong, on so many levels.

"I'm losing my mind a little bit, Jasper," I said as I walked him back to his house.

"Oh, well, as long as it's just a little bit, then."

"No, I'm seriously worried. I had nightmares all night. Woke up every hour. Went to the bathroom, back to bed, deep sleep, nightmares, awake, bathroom . . ."

"Wash, rinse, repeat."

"Then, this morning I woke up with this clear vision, a conviction, that everything would be okay again if I killed Mark Zuckerberg."

"Ha! You're telling me that of all the stuff you saw behind your father's big cyber curtain, the thing that has you freaked the most is that he is on *Facebook*?"

I had to wait several seconds for him to stop laughing.

"At least the other stuff is private," I say.

"Ah," he said, wiping a tear away, "you don't actually know that, though."

"Oh God."

"Would you calm down, please? You are fine. There's hardly anybody who hasn't fantasized about killing the big Z at one time or another. I'd say that's the last of the fantasies you need to be worrying about."

"Argghh," I said. "And you are my friend, why?"

"Don't ask me. It was your idea."

"What? How do you figure that?"

"Remember? You followed me down the railroad tracks that day?"

"That was *you*. Following *me*. Really freaked me out at first too."

"Yeah, well they're *my* tracks. If you didn't want to be followed, you shouldn't have been there."

I gave him a shove sideways, causing him to bounce off a chain-link fence guarding a scrubby front yard that didn't really need guarding. We were just reaching Jasper's house, down the raggedy, rickety old side street that seemed to have retired from active service along with the railroad line.

"I wouldn't even have bothered with you, except that you were the principal's kid and I thought that might do me some good. Fat chance there. Before, he didn't even know who I was. Now he stares at me like he caught me humping his garden gnomes."

"He doesn't have any garden gnomes."

"No, not anymore. You want to come up for dinner?" he asked, pointing up at the second-floor apartment of the triple-decker as if the height would be the decider.

"Oh, wow. Thanks," I said, looking up, then down, then across the street, then back toward home.

He tapped my shoulder. "I'll be needing an answer soon. I gotta go take a dump."

"No," I said quickly then. "That's really nice of you. But, when Dad's home, I like to have dinner with him. It's good for us, y'know. To eat together."

He shook his head, smilingly, as he crab-walked across his porch toward his bathroom up there on the second floor.

"You're a good boy, trying," he said.

I shrugged, started walking back my way.

"He shouldn't have to eat alone, if I'm around. We'll get used to each other again."

I was nearly home when my phone beeped a message. A rarity, it made me stop and dig to retrieve it.

It was Jasper: "Still on toilet. Thinkin' funny stuff. Like I be logging out here. Geddit? I just logged out. Made me wonder, did you remember to log out of dad computer? Hope so."

Ah, crap.

DESTINATION HOME

It is an extremely strange sensation.

I stayed with the ladies for as long as I possibly could, which meant ten o'clock. They have to be in the hostel by ten thirty or they get locked out, so I guess ten thirty is going to be my curfew too. Suits me just fine because what would I want to do after they were gone anyway? Nothing.

We sat on the beach, watched people, left the beach. We walked up and down Crystal City's streets, watched people. We all got hungry at the same time, so I told Molly that if she could take me to the best veal Parmesan sub in town then I was buying. I don't exactly have money to burn, and still need to budget while figuring out longer-term plans, but real hunger is a powerful influence on a guy. And squiring not just one but *two* nice ladies around town is an influence no man should want to resist.

It was a pretty good veal Parm. Molly had meatball, and Stacey had steak and cheese.

We went back to the beach, full and slow. We sat, we watched people again, and then it was ten.

When we split up at the junction where the bus station is, it was harder for me to leave than it was to leave each of my family homes. I think it was. It felt like it was.

Is this the alone-est I have ever been? I am thinking that as I navigate the streets between the station and my place.

Huh. My place.

I am thinking it as I take out the brass key on the moose-head ring and twirl it around my finger while I walk along streets already surprisingly familiar to me. In measurable ways, this is surely the most alone I have ever been. I left home. I flew blindly to this strange place. This strange-and-getting-stranger place. I told nobody, because when I reached that moment, the one from the movie scene when the fugitive just has to tell that special somebody or somebodies that he has to go and won't see them for a while but they will meet up again someday, there was nobody I felt like I could tell.

And I am thinking yes, this is the maximum of alone because my current two best friends are nipping home for curfew and really I don't even know those two best friends. But they said they would call me. Except I had to tell them that I am now off the grid. No phone, which I left in Dad's bathroom so he could hear it ring when he tried to call me and then he would finally take me seriously. No laptop, which is shiny and silver and new, which he bought me out of the black-and-blue because I couldn't very well be borrowing his, but which sat gleaming and prominent on the breakfast bar when I left.

These friends of mine could not call me, and so finding them was going to take concentrated effort, but that's the price of friendship and of disappearing and meaning it. Anybody can run and be found. That's no trick and it's no statement. Run, go and stay gone, that's real.

It's decided then, this is true alone, pure and undiluted, as I walk with my key swinging circles around my finger and I turn the last corner onto Syd's street.

It took only twenty minutes this time.

I turn the key in the lock, and of course my uncle Sydney has a well-oiled lock and the tumblers tumble all smooth and satisfying at my command.

I get inside, where the gleaming clean and comfortable house welcomes me. All mine, all new, all real.

All alone.

I sleep just as soundly on my second night in my father's brother's house as I did on the first. There is nobody trying to wake me in the morning, either, nobody bellowing or kicking my door, nobody comically knocking on my forehead.

So I wake gradually, listening to the birds outside my open window, hearing cars starting up for the morning commute. The weather outside already feels a little muggy, heavy on my tongue, although there is no sunshine to speak of.

I could lie here all day. Nobody, anywhere, is expecting anything of me.

There is a snap, and a thump at the front door and I jackknife up in the bed-sofa.

Then, there is nothing.

My heart rate quickens as I sit paralyzed for several seconds, realizing with quick clarity what I am living. I have restarted my life from scratch, new place, nobody knows me, and I know neither the place nor the people.

And I've moved in with my uncle the crime lord.

Jesus, anything could happen here. Why didn't it occur to me that *anything* could happen here? Is this what it's like being Sydney? Jumping up at every strange sound, never letting your guard down? Is this any way to live?

I'm listening hard for any kind of follow-up, and I do wish the birds would shut up now. I wish the traffic would start winding down rather than up, but still there is enough quiet in there that I can work out that nothing more seems to be happening around Sydney's front door.

If I am going to choose my life for myself, from all possible lives, then I have got to start choosing rather than just letting it happen to me. My stomach is still swirling, my arms and legs all twitchy, and nobody has my back. *Nobody.*

Is this what it's like to be Syd?

Is this any way to live?

Anything could happen here.

Hold on.

Anything could happen here.

That's right. It's all wide open now. Anything could happen.

That's what I came for.

Is this what it's like to be Syd? Of course not. Spend two minutes with the guy and you know he's not cowering in bed over things that go bump in the full light of day.

Is this any way to live? Of course it is, because it's better than any other way I know, and specifically because *anything could happen*.

I throw off my covers, and even though my heart has not stopped racing and I am already a little sweaty, I am not breaking stride, I am not backing up or slowing down, which is not the same as saying I have no fear of this lonesome unknown. It just means that I will go forward into it with my fear to keep me company.

My hearty stride would actually probably look like a joke to somebody witnessing me now, but I don't care because if I don't stride I might stop.

It's a package. It's come through the big, heavily sprung mail slot and fallen on the wood floor below, where it lies before me, in brown paper wrapping.

Is this what a bomb looks like? I realize I have no idea what a bomb through the mail might look like. Is that the kind of thing that happens in Syd's world, that people who want to get you get you with things stuffed through your letterbox? Does Syd have enemies and so therefore, do I have actual, honest-to-God enemies before I even have proper friends?

Enemies? I actually smile for a second. Scary, but a shitload cooler than Kevin Shitbag ever had in Ass Bucket.

Whatever it is, I can't leave it on the floor there for three more days or whatever until Syd gets back. Imagine the conversation? "What's that, Kev? When did it come? Why is it still there? The mail *frightened* you? Get outta my house."

I pick it up carefully, feeling maybe a couple pounds of weight, six by eight by two inches rectangular. I read somewhere how a letter bomb one quarter this size tore the whole second story off an auto body shop.

I turn it over.

It's addressed to *me*.

Letter bomb, indeed.

So, Dad knows I'm here. He wouldn't dare come to Syd's

place, though, I know that. Not unless he's developed some level of bravery or desperation he never had before.

I tear the package open as I sit on Syd's coffee table. There are perfectly comfortable furnishings all around me but before I had even realized what I was doing I had backed away from the front door as if it were booby-trapped, and plunked down with my parcel as soon as I felt the table bump the back of my knees. I am thinking I won't sit on tables when he's around, but he's not, and I pull the book out of the cardboard wrapping.

For crying out loud. He published it.

It's a copy of my father's poetry book. I knew the poems existed, individually, and he was always talking about the *collection*. God, the poems. He was always threatening to find a publisher, to get the whole mess assembled and between covers and out there in the world where they could embarrass everybody.

It embarrassed me every time he brought it up, but he hadn't done that in a very long time. And anyway, it was always just a joke. He was always laughing when he made that threat. Always laughing then.

The title of the collection is *Mind Monkeys*.

I do not open the thing. I look at the cover, which is glossy banana yellow with no artwork. It just has the title, followed by *A Cheeky Chapbook, by A. Chastened Chap.* Since the spine and back cover list my name as the publisher, we will assume either a monumentally freakish coincidence or self-publishing.

It's actually rather nicely done. He invested.

I drop it there on the coffee table and walk directly to *my* room in *my* home and pull on *my* clothes quickly. Then I go into *my* bathroom and brush *my* teeth. Then I march back, passing the living room, and its coffee table and its coffee-table book, without a look, swinging *my* key around *my* finger as I head out *my* door and into *my* life.

I know them all, every syllable, the correct meter, the singsong, the stresses, pauses, inflections. If he thinks he can make me cry remotely now, he is misfiguring Kiki Vandeweghe.

Circling behind the house, I discover a space in the hedge at the back of the small yard. That space opens up onto a scrubby bit of overgrown wildflower land, which I fight through until I emerge onto the Little League diamond.

It's empty of kids, this field. I pause for a few seconds and think this is maybe one of those moments when I would get a little thoughtful and misty in light of all my changes and look back on my Little League days fondly or sadly or whatever.

I never had any Little League days.

I step across the field, and reach the chain-linked basketball court where one lone skinny gawky guy is shooting lazy baskets with no enthusiasm at all.

I never played basketball.

I move on, beyond the court and past the tennis court. I played some tennis. I liked it, way back then, when things were likeable. I might try it again sometime.

I walk on through a small thicket of pines and onto the path that runs beside the river that turns out to be a canal and takes me where it is I am meant to go.

Poetry, for shit's sake. Where does he think he's going with that?

The girls and I agreed that if I have to be *so* mysteriously below the radar then I could just try to catch up with them at Crystal Beach right after they are done with church any given morning. It is all casual, and all casual is what I am all about.

I do not feel casual, as I hotstep it along the canal towpath. The walk is great, cool-ish and quiet with the sluggish water meandering along on my left side and a fair amount of greenery along my right. I'm a little too frothy in the head to slow down and appreciate it just now, but I know that eventually I will. The canal leads down to the beach, and after about a mile and a quarter, I see it opening up before me.

I am hoping hard the girls are going to show up, and I

feel, actually, stunned and stupid about how much I want to see them.

Yet because this place I'm in is so foreign and new to me, I am something like glad, something like relieved, when I hit the beach and see groupings of folks, characters, who, dodgy though they may be, look familiar to me. The weak wave motion of the water slurps at the shore and I find that inviting. I head for it, scanning for Stacey and Molly as I do. It's an overcast day, hot again away from the trees, and there aren't enough people hanging out for them to go unnoticed. They're not here.

So I guess for now I'm just like everyone else around here, killing time until they come.

Crystal Beach could use a cleanup, that's for sure. It's not public-health-hazard stuff yet, but it wouldn't take too many more cigarette packs, junk-food wrappers, or disposable diapers to tip the balance. I walk along it, starting at the canal mouth. It feels like my own personal grand entrance onto the beach as the towpath could pretty much lead me blindfolded straight from Syd's backyard to here. The path is actually much neater than the beach, looking like somebody is responsible for the upkeep, whacking the invasive greenery back and picking up the litter.

I did the groundskeeping around our house.

Nobody does it on Crystal Beach.

Sprouts of very rugged-looking weeds pop up out of the ground randomly, all the way down to the shoreline. There, some other species climb up out of the bay water, seeming like the gnarly green hands of a bunch of somebodies trapped below and desperately trying to get out. The water itself looks surprisingly clear, though between the unusual odor and sinister sea foliage it would take a braver man than me to swim it.

We had a pool, back home. It was just a small one. I was responsible for that, too. I did a good job.

I walk the couple hundred yards of navigable frontage until the marshland gives way to much denser, wildly overgrown grasses, weeds, and vines that serve as a natural break between the wasteland of Crystal Beach and the grubby productivity of the wharves just beyond. The small wavelets lap and slurp all the way, keeping me whispery company, which is certainly welcome. One tugboat crosses the harbor right to left, and one ancient trawler—looking like some mutant, clawed sea creature itself—passes the opposite way. The air does not move at all. The sea and sky are joined in that color moment when stainless and blue steel meet.

Then it ends. I stand like a dope, waiting for instructions. Unsurprisingly, none come.

I turn and walk back the way I came, over the same gritty sand, past the same wreckage of a big, double baby stroller, through the same wonderful stretch of about thirty yards that is untouched by any clutter or mess at all, no weeds, no garbage, even the sand itself seems to be of a finer grade than the rest and almost groomed. I walk those thirty yards quite slowly.

Yet, even as I step again onto the tired sand, the sad sand with the blemishes and dog shit, I listen to the slurping sound this beach produces, and it makes me foolishly happier.

That slurp is Crystal Beach's voice. It's a singular thing. I can think it's speaking to me directly and I can think we understand one another.

That is a poetry I can get.

I don't think the pool and I ever understood one another.

I am lost in this understanding when a Frisbee thumps me in the chest.

"Yo, adorable," yells Mickey, the guy who throated me with the Frisbee the first time. He still has the long frayed cutoffs on, but now he's also sporting a giant mint-green short-sleeved linen shirt that as I approach I realize smells like he took it off a big fat dead guy. A *long*-dead fat guy.

"So, I'm adorable today," I say, picking the Frisbee up and walking it over to him.

"What're you, *sensitive* or somethin'? Thin skin like that, my man, and you won't last a week livin' on these streets."

"What?" I say, indignant and helping prove his point. "I'm not *homeless*."

"Ahhh . . . !" he blurt-laughs and points at me while turning around to perform for his pals. Now I have to be his straight man, and Jesus, I wish Stacey were here already. "You hear the way Prince Fancypants here says that word, 'homeless'? Like he swallowed a fat creamy maggot or somethin'."

I don't help my case further by gagging slightly at the thought. More laughter.

"Okay, so what're you doing here alone slinkin' around our beach like you're some kind of freak? You some kinda freak, boy?"

It seems right away like this is the kind of thing a guy's got to quash immediately or live with forever.

"I'm no kinda freak, and I wasn't slinkin'. I just like the ocean, is that a crime?"

Now Mickey looks for the first time as if I've truly puzzled him. He points out toward the horizon. "You mean, *that*? You really are lost, ain't ya. That ain't the ocean, junior, that's the ocean's *backwash*."

I do wonder how many of these stomach-churning analogies he's got in his bag of tricks, but I do not want to test it out.

"It's not so bad," I say, looking away from him and out toward the unloved bay. "It just needs a little more appreciation, that's all."

"Did I *say* we don't appreciate it, ass funnel?"

I guess I can't help testing it.

"No, I suppose you didn't, but—"

"That's right, I didn't. We do appreciate it. In fact, we appreciate it enough that we don't let just any scrote-face freak think he can trespass on our beach without permission or authorization or paying of proper respects . . ."

More than at any time since I slammed the door on my old house and my old everything, I feel at this moment like I am where I do not belong.

Which is exactly where I want to be. Which is exactly what I came for.

"I'm with Stacey," I say with a shaky unconvincing bravado, "and Molly. Remember? So, I'm not—"

"Oh, what, Jesus's baby sister? Try finding somebody who *hasn't* been with that little wombat."

"What?" I say, too startled, too obvious. "Come on now, that's kinda—"

"That other one, though, the tall one, she might be worth a go. You tappin' that?"

"What?" I repeat that same unwise surprise, but this time I catch it and try to improve on it. "Ah, I think that's the kind of thing a gentleman doesn't talk about."

"You kiddin' me? Half the reason the gentleman even does it is so he can talk about it."

If I get any farther back on my heels in this conversation, I'll be on my elbows.

"Stacey's a friend," I say. I like the sound as it rolls out of me. Where *is* she?

"Right, fine, whatever, you don't really know me or any of the other guys and so you don't want to share your booty. That's cool. Maybe after we get to know each other better and we're all buds and brothers, you'll share the booty around like good friends do."

Am I supposed to answer that? Was there even a question in there?

Mickey stares at me like I'm something unidentifiable that the backwash washed up. My lack of responsiveness eventually gets to him and he fills the void.

"You smoke?" he says, reaching into his fat-dead-guy shirt pocket and pulling out a joint about the size of my middle finger.

"Sure I smoke, time to time."

Time to time meaning one time when I was a freshman and got a proximity wasting on the bus, and once two years later when four guys from the football team got ahold of me late on a dark November afternoon after we all had detention. They surrounded me and blew me a shotgun high when I politely declined a more sociable one. That was also on a bus. Buses made me woozy for weeks after that.

But this time, I won't be forced or accidentalized, because that stuff doesn't happen to Kiki.

"Here ya go, my man," says the man. So the same guy who hit me with the Frisbee on my first time to Crystal Beach, and again on my second, is now hitting me with the biggest joint I have ever been able to see and smell and partake of of my own free will. Surely this represents progress.

"So, how you know that li'l freak Molly?" Mickey asks as he gives up the smoke.

I answer quickly, before actually smoking anything, because I'm not sure I'll be able afterward. "I don't *know* her, know her. We just met, really. At the bus station."

"Uh-hooo," he says. He is joined now by a couple of his pals, attracted instantly by the smoke. They waste no time joining in the hooting of me. I take a pull on the joint, cautiously. "So," he adds, laughing. "You one of *them* freaks."

The accusation, whatever it is, shocks me even before the smoke does. I try to protest and defend my honor and process the smoke all at once. With limited success, it must be said.

"Wait, what, no-ho—," I say, and I dissolve in a spasm of fit-coughing that jerks me forward, hard and repeatedly, as if I am being tased and given a tracheotomy simultaneously. The guys are having a hell of a time with my show, as they should, until Mickey finally takes it seriously enough to come over and start slapping my back with one hand and shoving something like Gatorade under my nose with the other.

I throw back the Gatorade, and throw it right back up again.

The gang could hardly be enjoying me more. I've never been such a big hit.

It's several minutes before I can rejoin the conversation. The other guys have continued without me, kept on smoking and drinking and so are well oiled for my return.

"What's your name, anyway, dude?" Howard asks.

"Kiki Vandeweghe," I say proudly with my new hard rasp of a smokehouse voice.

"Whoa," Mickey says. "That's a hot shit of a name."

"It's Dutch," I say, sitting back on a log now because standing seems kind of complicated. "Both my parents are Dutch. They sent me here to go to school. Boarding school in New York. Then Exeter."

I was thinking that was one of my best bits. A little stoned, I was thinking it was can't-miss. I was thinking erroneously.

"I said it was a cool name," Mickey says. "Shut up and don't ruin it, huh?"

"Sorry," I say.

"Don't be sayin' 'sorry.' You sound like a weenie. You don't want to be weenying around here, trust me."

"Right. Right."

"Anyway, this is Howard, and this is Tailbone. He's called Tailbone because he's just above asshole, but not by much."

"Shut *up* with that shit already," Tailbone says, taking the Frisbee and biffing Mickey across the head with it. "You know that's not why. It's because of all the tail that I—"

"Kiki Vandeweghe is not interested in your sad little fantasy life," Mickey says.

Well, actually, stoned Kiki is pretty interested in it.

"What kind of freak are you talking about?" I ask. "With the Molly thing, I mean."

Howard cuts in. "You know, man. The fishin'-for-holy-trolls-online type. It's all, 'Nice Christian girl looking to meet nice Christian fella. Meet me at the bus station for prayer meeting and possibly some born-again ass-pumping.'"

"Oh God," I say.

"Yeah," Howard says, pointing at me, "she says that a lot. Screams it, in fact. That's why she's the Godfucker."

I can't stand the fact that this sounds so harrowing and unreal to me even as these guys fall all over the place laughing. Is this stuff funny? Is this what counts for comedy out here? This is somebody's life being ridiculed to hell, or, to . . . wherever. A perfectly nice little somebody as far as I can tell. I have to believe the weed is doing the laughing for them because nobody could find this kind of stuff funny, could they?

So why am I laughing along as heartily as any of them?

It's the drug. It has to be. It cannot be me, because I am better than this. I am, aren't I?

• • •

"Your friends ain't comin'," Mickey says after around forty minutes lying in the sand, watching the sun melt away the clouds, and waiting.

"How do you know?" I say.

"Because I know every damn thing," he says convincingly.

"It's true," Howard adds, "he does."

"Oh," I say. "Damn."

"Don't take it personal," Tailbone says. "Everything's fast-moving parts around here, 'cause it's gotta be. You say you're supposed to meet someone somewhere, sometime, and maybe they got arrested or dead or married or somethin' and you could just never know what really went down. Never see 'em again and you're none the wiser as to why."

"So you never think it's about you, or you go nuts," Mickey says.

"Except," Howard says, "in your case it probably is you."

"Yeah, it's you," adds Tailbone.

"Nice guys," I say.

That must be the right response because Howard lets out a whoop of victory.

"We are nice guys," Mickey adds. "And we're your friends now, right? You can never have enough friends out here. Everything is temporary. That's the reality that you have to deal with. You want your numbers for when you need people behind you. You'll see your girls again, I'm sure. But because you seem like an all-right dude you also have us. We got your back, and doesn't it feel like you're a very lucky dude indeed?"

It does. It very much does.

So much so that if I dare try to express how foolishly lucky and happy this does make me, it will be a creepshow and probably earn me a beating.

"Cool," I say, because that's me being cool. "Now, sign my cast, will you?"

"Of course," Mickey says, and the three of them come bumping up a little uncomfortably close.

I feel kind of slick as I pull out my new flashy Montblanc pen. And even though it takes a whole lot more scratching than my cheapo marker does to make a decent mark on a cast, this is now my writing instrument of choice.

"Whoa-ho," Mickey says, turning the beautiful lacquered thing all around, examining the gold tip really close, holding it to the brightening sky. "This is a gorgeous little piece of work, Mr. Kiki." He grins at me and starts scraping his signature into the plaster. "That's real gold too, bitch."

"Thanks," I say proudly, like I made it myself or something.

He passes it on to Howard, who grunts as he attempts to make his mark.

"You're a man who likes quality stuff," Mickey says.

"Sure," I say, though not really sure.

"That's a nice watch, too."

"Yeah?" I say, looking at it anew. "It's okay, yeah. I got it for . . . yeah, it's all right. Nothing special, really."

Mickey smiles at me in a cheesy way that I don't get, but I figure a smile is a smile these days whether I quite understand it or not and so I return-smile back at him.

"This thing sucks," Tailbone barks, shoving the pen back at me. "I need something else if you want my signature."

I take back the Montblanc and pull the stubby marker out of my other pocket. Mickey and I shake our heads and shrug at silly, clueless Tailbone, who does not understand finer things like we do.

JASPER JEALOUS

He gave you a present?" Jasper asked when he saw my new laptop.

"I wouldn't call it a present, exactly."

"No, of course you wouldn't. A normal person, with sense and gratitude and no persecution complex, however, would call it a present. And a pretty fine one at that. Especially considering you were essentially rewarded for skulking around his house and spying on him in a particularly icky manner."

We were walking along the abandoned tracks on our way home from school for the last time this year. There was one day of the term left, but it was a Friday, and thus fell outside of Jasper's walking schedule. He had by now dimmed some of the shine off my presentation, though not off the computer itself, which gleamed.

"I was not skulking," I said, slipping the thing back into my backpack. "And any ickiness involved was down to him, not me. I think maybe that's why he didn't say a word about it. Not one word."

"You win again. Like always."

"Uh-huh. And, shut up. Like always."

We had reached the turnoff, where he would head down his street and I would continue on to my place.

"So," he said, "what you up to now?"

"Nothing," I said, shrugging.

"Wanna do something?" he asked.

"Sure," I said. "Want to come over? I can show you all the cool stuff my new computer can do."

"Sure, happy to come. But can I play on your father's machine instead? That way by tomorrow he'll have to buy me one too."

"Um, he's just starting to remember how to have one son, so maybe we won't overload him just yet."

"Okay, but we'll work me in eventually. Anyway, on the subject of you two getting back into some kind of groove, what's the summer looking like?"

We had reached sight of my house by now, and I noticed someone unfamiliar on the porch.

"I have no idea," I said, focusing on the person, a woman. "But it's what I've been looking forward to. With him off for the summer just like me, I figure this is going to be our time. It has to be, doesn't it? I'm sure we'll start talking about it today or tomorrow."

"This is good," he said. "Very promising."

We reached the steps of the house and the woman turned to us as we mounted them.

"Hello," she said pleasantly.

"Can I help you?" I asked.

"Well, yes. I was supposed to meet somebody here, maybe that would be your father?"

"Maybe that would be," I said cautiously. I wasn't sure whether the situation called for me to be happy for him, conflicted over the next step in the whole *moving on* progression, or what. She was quite pretty, though, and polite, so I was leaning in the direction of giving my approval.

"He should be here soon," I said. "Can I ask what this is about?"

"Oh, of course," she said, "I'm sorry, I should have said. I'm Michelle Simon. I'm renting the house for the summer?" She did that thing of making the last statement sound like a question when I obviously didn't recognize her name. But it was no question.

"Hi, Michelle," Jasper said, taking her hanging hand when it became apparent I wasn't up to the job. "I'm Jasper, and this is Kevin. He lives here."

"Well, not as of next week," she said lightheartedly, even poking me in the ribs. She thought it would be a fun moment for both of us, since she was looking forward to cozying up in our house while my dad and I were surely off on some wonderful adventure that we would both remember for the rest of our lives.

WHAT'S YOUR FREAKERY

I wake up to poking.

"Hey," says the smart, small voice with the bubble in the throat. "What are you doing here?" She's poking me with the toe of her shoe as I roll over in her direction and see that it's light out. I have definitely been sleeping. My left side is clammy cold, from the sand, which has melded with the drool stream leaking from the left corner of my mouth to form a kind of sand-castle paste that sticks as I get my face upright.

It takes me many seconds of being upright and listening to my special slurping surf to get it all together and answer Molly's question sufficiently.

"I was waiting for you," I say.

"Oh, get out," she says, grinning. "You were never."

It comes clearer to me every second. "Yes, I was."

"You were waiting for Stacey, maybe."

"I was waiting for both of you," I say, and start to scan the beach for clues.

The night has passed, and the day has come. The only conscious residents of Crystal Beach right now are myself and Molly, though there are plenty of bodies splayed around, which may or may not still possess heartbeats and souls. If they ever possessed souls. There is a nice soft-glow peach of a sunrise peaking its fuzzy head above the horizon and making Crystal's backwash backwater look as magical as any real-world beach.

My summer holiday paradise.

I remember waiting. When Mickey and the boys decided to head out for adventures elsewhere and I declined the invitation because I was sure the girls would be here momentarily. I remember the sun getting stronger through the afternoon and into the evening, and the greenflies skewering and lancing me until I hollered, and then Mickey returning with quarts of malt liquor and even bigger spliffs and apples and tortilla chips, and they really were my friends, these guys.

"That's sweet of you," Molly says, and she appears to get far more overcome about it than necessary. She has to wipe both of her big eyes with both of her little hands. It makes me uneasy enough that I reach out and take both of those small hands in my medium-size ones. Her cast is about ten times as dirty as mine, and it smells a little.

"So, where is Stacey?" I ask.

"Back at the hostel, I guess," she says.

"Shouldn't you be there with her?"

She inhales deeply, snuffles.

"I was late. Curfew. Locked out. I had someplace to be. And then I didn't. It happens sometimes."

"Couldn't you call Stacey to let you in?"

"Oh, I couldn't wake her. And I wouldn't want to get her in trouble. It was my fault, so it's my problem. I know the rules—be out of the building between eight a.m. and eight p.m. except on days when they're working you. And ten thirty lockout."

"Molly? That means you can't get back in until eight o'clock tonight?"

"Well, church is at eight this morning. So, I thought I'd sit in there for a while. It's a nice church. Seats are kinda hard, though."

Molly looks away, looks even smaller and weaker than her usual self. She starts working herself down into the dirty sand like she's settling in, like a crab hiding in the shallows. It's chilly now, I can feel it in my joints.

"What are you here for now?" I ask.

"Sleep," she says, and works her way farther down into the ground.

I look all around the beach, at the characters sleeping or just lying in wait, at the orangey sun rising and shining them into view.

"Don't you worry that something could happen to you?"

"You didn't worry when you slept here."

"I didn't sleep, I passed out."

"And look at you. You're fine."

"I'm lucky. You can't always be lucky."

She continues crabbing herself down into the dirty sand. Then she shrugs. "I'm not new at this, Kiki. I know how to take care of myself."

I'm sure she does not.

"I'm sure you do, Molly. But you can't control everything. Or everybody."

"Well, I sort of can. Times before, somebody started hassling me, we just always worked something out. It's just how it goes. It's fine."

I realize that only one of us is at all disturbed by this, but the one is disturbed about it enough for everybody. Molly has her eyes closed already and she looks like a kid falling asleep in a chair in front of a TV, home, warm, and safe.

How does this happen? How is this in any way *fine*?

And what kind of guy *allows* it to happen?

"My father is a poet," I say to her quiet face, just as her helmet-head of sponge hair tips back and collects a pound of sand.

Molly perks up, half-emerging from her little nest and looking more interested than poetry should ever warrant.

"Really?" she asks. "Really, he is? That's special. That is a very unusual thing, a father who is a poet. That's something, and I bet you are like, wow, proud about it. He must be gentle, like a poet. That's where you get it, obviously, all that gentle."

Nobody is gentle.

"You want to see his book?" I ask.

She nods wildly, vigorously, and honestly. I stand up and offer her my good left hand.

I take Molly along the canal route, which she says she normally tries to avoid.

"You better be careful," she says. "This path can be very dangerous."

"I know how to handle myself," I say, not even sure whether I'm joking or not.

Molly is sure, and laughs out loud.

"You don't know how to handle yourself. It's part of your charm."

"No, it isn't." I start to pull my hand away from hers, but

she grabs tight and she is shockingly strong. The cartilage in my hand crunches.

"Well, it is. You're just so nice. Is that your freakery, the niceness?"

"I'm not that nice. And, *what*?"

"Come on, everybody has their freakery. Their *thing*," she says, accompanying the word with a shoulder-hunching, lip-snarling, tongue-dangling visual that really requires nothing more for explanation. "Hyper-niceness, some people get off on it, some people get lucky with it. Then you can nicey-nicey girls along the garden path—or the towpath—to the place where the chainsaw is waiting, is that it?"

This is sickening me every which way and this time I do wrench my hand from her grip. She giggles.

"Is that what you think?" I ask.

"I don't know. I don't even know you, do I?"

"And yet," I say, my voice rising in frustration, "here you are, with me. On the towpath."

Molly smiles and shakes her head in wonder, like we are discussing some newly discovered life form rather than her own actual self.

"I'm not renowned as a fine judge of character," she says, slamming us both at the same time.

"No, but you are renowned as a Godfucker," I say, bitter nasty and instantly ashamed of it.

Her smile drops right off her face, down to her little shoes and into the canal.

Through it all, though, we keep walking.

"I guess I am," she says. "But hey, I'm *renowned*, right?"

"I'm sorry, Molly," I say, taking her left hand again. Remarkably, she lets me. Where does somebody acquire such tolerance, forgiveness? "See, I'm not so nice after all."

"Pffft," she says, swinging my hand as we approach the trees by the courts and the baseball field. "That's you being not nice? I just thought you were coming on to me."

She is resilient, I must give her that.

Let's hope I can learn a thing or two from her. Because if Sydney finds out, I'll be ass-whipped *and* homeless.

But he won't. There's no way he will be home for another day or two at least. And this is just a short visit, a humanitarian thing. The right thing. A fine thing.

And I will clean every last spot.

"That's me," I say, pointing up at my window as we cross the field and scoot through the hedge.

"Sweet," Molly says, looking up and then all around. "You have a yard and everything. A basement bulkhead. I thought basement bulkheads were outlawed after the one in *The Wizard of Oz* flew up and conked Dorothy in the head."

Feeling a bit clever, I say, "Oh no, now, would a nice guy

like me have an uncle with an illegal basement bulkhead?"

We are standing, admiring my window. It's a one-level ranch house, but the backyard slopes away so it feels like we are looking up at something bigger.

"Did you just say something kinky?" she asks, and does appear to wonder.

Only about my uncle's criminality.

"Ah, no," I say, and look down. The grass needs cutting. "And I don't believe I've ever met anybody who thinks quite like you do."

"No," she says flatly, "you haven't. Now, am I gonna get to see your window from the other side, or is this it?"

I lead her around to the front of the house. I whip out my key and wave it in front of her, as if a mere house key is something mystical and precious to anybody else.

"Um, okay, I get it, Kiki," she says, then goes all brighty. "Oh, right. Kiki. Key-Key, very cute, very amusing, very sad."

I hadn't thought of that at all, but I don't have an explanation that'll make me look any better for getting all excited over having my own key, so I leave it alone and open the door.

"This place is amazing," she says, rushing through the door and doing a dancer's twirl in the hallway. She flits through the living room and kitchen, doing another spin at each stop. "I have never *seen* a place so sparkling clean. And it looks like a diner. This place is killer."

"Ah, well, thanks," I say, happy to take any credit available.

She scuttles along, checking all the rooms, and goes for Syd's bedroom before I can stop her.

"This one's locked," she says.

"Yes," I confirm.

"Is it *your* room, you ol' kinkster? Does that magic key of yours open this one?"

"No. And no. That's my uncle's room."

"Right, then, all the dungeon stuff is in there, and your doghouse and choker collar and stuff, right?"

I don't know how to stop her, but I can at least not encourage this.

"No, Molly. Those things are not in there."

"They're in the basement, then? Behind the *bulkhead of screams*?"

I sigh. "There is no bulkhead of screams."

She giggles crazily at the sound of me saying the things she made up. I suppose it does sound funny when I say it.

She walks to the bathroom, flips on the light, and reacts as if Jesus himself is squatting on the throne in there.

"Jesus, Mary, and Joseph," she says, so maybe it's the whole family.

I scoot over to where she stands. "What is it?"

"It's so . . . white. It's like, glowing."

"Well," I say, looking around, nodding, "it is porcelain and tile."

"Well, I myself have never seen such clean. It even . . ." She takes a good long inhale. "It even smells better than regular air, never mind toilet air. I think this is a dummy, and the real bathroom is somewhere else because I seriously doubt any assness has ever been done in here."

I laugh. "It's a clean place. The proprietor takes it seriously."

"Well, my compliments to the proprietor. Or I'll tell him myself when I see him."

"I'll tell him," I snap, edgy enough to draw an arched eyebrow from Molly.

Suddenly, she grabs my arm and starts pulling, pleading. "Oh, Kiki, can I take a shower? Please, please? I would die to have a shower here. The ones at the hostel are old and grotty and the mold doesn't come away no matter how hard we scrub. I feel just as germy coming out as I did going in. And there are no locks on the doors so anybody can come in whenever they want to and I just can't relax because I have the spooks about that and feel the whole time like I'm the star of one of those shower slasher horror movies and I am about to get it in the neck any second. I mean it, I wash myself so fast and furious that sometimes the soap shoots right out of my hand and up and over the curtain rod and I hear it bounce on the floor on the other side. And then, of course, that's it, because no way am I going out after that soap when you-know-who with the big slasher knife is waiting for me to do just that because that was his plan."

I just stand there, watching her blink and hyperventilate as if she is in fact exactly that slasher shower horror actress.

"Have a shower, Molly."

I go over and slide the glass door open, work the taps and get it going just right, when I turn back to find her standing naked and staring excitedly, right past me to the glory that is Uncle Sydney's antiseptic temple of clean.

"*Molly*," I gasp, like somebody's great aunt.

"Oh, please," she says, brushing, nakedly, past me and stepping in, "you're family."

She smacks the shower door closed and immediately and audibly begins appreciating the moment of bliss.

"Don't get your cast wet?" I say in a voice suddenly unrecognizably high as I step over the small mound of Molly things on the floor.

"Don't get yours wet either," she says, giggling. Giggling.

I rush out and slam that bathroom door, as confused and conflicted as I have been since I was thirteen. Only then I was slamming from the other side of the bathroom door. And actually I wasn't anywhere near this conflicted.

• • •

I am in the kitchen, chopping up apples, nectarines, and kiwi into a bowl, about to pour yogurt over it all, when Molly strolls in. It's been about forty-five minutes. She has a big thick white bathrobe on and the shower has done something remarkable to her skin that makes it look like she's generating her own soft amber light from inside her chest somewhere.

"I hope you don't mind. I found this in that bathroom cupboard. My clothes disgusted me by the time I got back to them."

Not sure how my voice is going to perform, so I just wave the knife around in what I hope is a recognizable, no-problem manner.

"Well, as far as knife-wielding shower slashers go, I don't think you'll be giving me any nightmares."

"Ha," I say, and that one syllable sounds reliably me enough to go for speech. "I'm making you a little something. . . ."

"Oh," she says, "that is so kind. I think, though, that I'm not going to be able to eat anything before I sleep. I just can't . . ."

"Oh, that's fine," I say. "I'll just keep it in the fridge for you."

She shakes her head at me, smiling warmly. "If this is your freakery, boy, you do some pretty fine freakery."

"Watch it now," I say, menacing her with the knife in an unmenacing way.

I lead her to my sofa-bedroom. "That shower was the

best, best thing that ever happened to me, Kiki. Thank you. I think I might want to take another one when I wake up."

I see on the way past that her Molly mound is still on the bathroom floor.

"I can throw your things in the wash if you like," I say.

She sits down on my bed, then lies down, all fluid motion and purr.

"You want to keep me company?" she says.

"Oh," I say. "Oh, I would love . . . I think, though, that maybe you should . . ."

"You just, if you don't mind, if you could be quick about it because I'm really exhausted and everything."

"What? No. What? No. I wouldn't . . ."

"It's only fair," she says calmly. "You don't want to?"

Oh dear God, I do.

"No," I say, "I don't."

She is puzzled, and quite rightly, too.

"Why? What's wrong?"

This is wrong.

"Nothing's wrong. It's just, I want you to know that everybody's not like that. I'm not like those other guys."

I am, though. I am, damn. I am.

"Sure you are," she says, smiling and nestling down catlike deep into the covers. "But that's okay, it's not your fault. You can't help it."

"I'm not." I am. "You're wrong." She's right. "Now, sleep."

I walk briskly toward the door.

"Aren't you going to read me a poem?" she calls.

Hell shit anyway. Almost got away.

"You know," she says in a voice sleepier by the second, "the poetry book. That your father wrote."

"Yeah, ah, about that . . ."

"The book that you invented as a ploy to get me to your creepy lair, and the basement bulkhead of screams and all that?"

I almost prefer to tell her that she's got it exactly right and I did all that vile stuff, rather than confess that my father's book is here, and if I read from it, I could well burst into tears. She would probably find this endearing and I would be further mortified and humiliated and not at all the man I wanted to be when I arrived in this life, thus destroying everything. He's between those covers, hiding inside to trap me. I haven't been able to open the thing, never mind *read out loud from it to a girl*. Kiki cannot do that.

"I'll be right back," I say, and walk the long mile to the living room and coffee table and book, then the long, long mile back again. By the time I return to my room I still haven't cracked *Mind Monkeys* open to even the title page, and I swear I can feel the binding actually buzzing in my hand.

"Right, Molly, here's the thing," I say, and look across my room to find her sleeping soundly. Way to go, poetry, the one art form that can put you to sleep before it even enters the room. I lay the book down next to the bed, and slip back out again.

I feel kind of parental as I go quietly about and collect Molly's things from the bathroom floor, but parental has me all conflicted again so I'll just think of myself as the help for now. I empty out the pockets of her cutoff jeans and dump the contents on the top of the washer. Cell phone, Halls Mentho-Lyptus extra-strong throat lozenges, only two remaining. Enough small-change coinage that if she went out swimming she would sink and her petite self would never be found.

I stuff the stuff into the washer, throw in some powder, and set it off to the races.

I *am* a good guy. I *can* think about somebody else for a change. So there, Jasper, you missed it. I did all that despite nobody even watching. And I didn't do anything else, either, no overhandling the girly merchandise or any of that kinkster malarkey, despite nobody even watching.

There, I went and did it now. Thinking about what I didn't do. Girly merchandise. I should go to the bathroom now if I'm going to congratulate myself any further.

I'm catching a few badly needed winks myself, sitting in Syd's wingback reading chair with my feet up on the ottoman, when I hear the alarm beep saying the clothes are dry. There has been no sign, through washing and drying cycles, that Molly is stirring at all. I go out to the kitchen, take the things out, along with a couple of kitchen towels that had already been sitting in there.

Would a gentleman fold? Which would be more noble? To be manhandling her things by folding? Or to hand them over all balled up, which sounds bad but preserves modesty?

I realize the reason I even have the clothes is that she shed them right there in front of me. Somehow it doesn't help me decide. Doesn't help me form thoughts at all, in fact.

Molly's phone goes off, making me jump and drop the white blouse on the floor before I can do anything with it. Her ring tone is "Ave Maria," and lying on top of the washer's metal skin, it reverberates like a washer-dryer-size phone, rumbly. I snap it up to quiet it and see on the screen that the call is from Stacey.

Should be fun.

"Hello," I whisper, partly out of respect for the sleeper, and partly to be all deceptive and sultry.

"You were not at church, bitch," she says. "And you didn't come home last night, which means you needed church all the more."

"God?" I say. "Is that you, God? How did you find me here? Right, it was the omnipotence thing again, wasn't it?"

Stacey's voice drops two octaves and about forty degrees. "Who is this? Is Molly all right? Where is she? Cocksucker, if you did anything to harm that girl, I'm gonna slice your—"

"Stacey, Stacey," I say, in a little bit of hysterics and a lot of fear, "it's me. Kiki."

There is a pause that is long enough to make me think we've lost the connection. Then her voice comes back just about the same depth and temperature as before. "She was with *you* last night?"

"Well, that's not exactly what . . . hey. Was that shock I just heard? How come you said it like that? Like her being with *me* was such a bizarre idea?"

"Well, ah. You know . . ."

She doesn't have a ready answer. Stacey doesn't have a smart-ass, hard-boiled retort to stop me in my tracks there and I am not pleased about it. Am I that bad?

"So, I'm that bad."

"No, no, you're not. Not at all. I didn't mean anything like . . . wait a minute. Did you do the God thing? Oh, for shit's sake, Kiki, tell me, please, tell me you did not do the God thing just to make this happen."

That sounds so truly awful. I didn't even do it and I feel like a scumbag just for making it into the conversation.

"Should I be offended, Stacey?"

"I would hope so."

"Well, I am offended."

"Oh, thank God. You are the good one, aren't you, Kiki?"

"Now I'm unoffended. I like that. Not even *one-of-the-good-ones,* but *the* . . ."

"Oh, too right. You are the only one. If you are."

"Harsh."

"Yup. So where's our girl?"

"Right now, she's in my bed."

There's that dead air again.

"Hello? Stace—"

"What's she doing there if you didn't God-up, *Vandeweghe*?"

Yikes. It's only a phone call and still I feel in physical jeopardy.

"She's sleeping, *Dimbleby*." I figure she has to respect my standing up to her that much.

"Tell me you didn't really believe my actual name was Anastasia Dimbleby."

I should probably just take the Fifth on this one.

"That answers that, then. So tell me, what are you doing, while the princess slumbers?"

"I . . . well, if you must know, I was doing her laundry."

"Her lau . . . ? Are you lying?"

"Why would I lie about that?"

"So you did take her home, you slithery male serpent, you. But then you did her laundry."

I give that statement a quick once-over and decide it is sufficiently factual-based that I can sign off on it without elaboration or detraction and it will do my reputation no harm whatsoever on all counts.

"That is correct," I say, trying to sound like this is just another day at the office for me.

"Well," she says, "now I'm not sure whether to slice you up from 'nads to neckline, or find a way to clone your strange ol' self."

"Do I get a vote?" I say.

"No. But I'm sure I'll have it figured out one way or the other by the time I see you."

"Oh good. That's a relief."

"Is she really sleeping?" Stacey asks.

"I'm pretty sure. I could check in."

"Yeah, you probably should. If she misses any more curfews she's gonna lose her place here and be back out on the street. And also I don't know how I would last here in Godtown without Molly to draw all their repent-and-be-saved fire."

I walk toward my bedroom, still whispering.

"Well, Sister Stacey, she's feeling much better and she's got her uniform all washed and nice for school again."

"Did you remember to use fabric softener?"

"Actually, I did."

"Of course you did, weirdo. Good thing. That outfit was getting kinda rank."

"Not as rank as the cast, though."

"Arggh, I know. I think she was supposed to get it off something like three weeks ago, but she's got some kind of peculiar mental emotional attachment to it. We'll work on it somehow."

"Good," I say, gently pushing open my door.

"Did you just tell me I'm good?" Molly says, looking up all dewey-eyed at me. She appears sincere in her question. She also seems sincere with the tears welling up.

"Absolutely," I say to Molly.

"Absolutely what?" Stacey says.

"Absolutely, Molly is good," I say. "And she is awake."

I hand the phone to Molly. She is all sniffles as she takes it and then shushes me away sternly.

"Listen to this, Stacey," she says, the bubbles rising in her voice and falling from her eyes as she starts to read.

Christ. The poems.

When Molly finally comes out of *her* room, she's wearing the white fluffy bathrobe and great, puffy, sore, saucer eyes.

"You all right?" I say.

"Sure. Just crying."

"Stacey, right? She can be tough. Don't take it so hard. She nearly made me cry just before you—"

"Stacey didn't make me cry. I made *her* cry if you wanna know the truth."

"Stacey?"

"Stacey."

"You. Made Stacey. Cry. Stacey?"

"Stacey. Except it wasn't me, really. It was your dad."

"Aw shit," I say, and jump back as she draws the poetry book out of the bathrobe. "He's toxic. Like ammonia mixed with whatever it is you're not supposed to mix ammonia with. He makes everybody cry."

"You don't have to be such a *guy* about it," she says, eventually laying the book on top of the washer-dryer. "They're stunning. I read every one. Such a soft soul. They have great spirituality, really. Do you have a favorite? You must have."

"Ah, yeah, the one that goes, 'There once were three twins from Toledo . . .'"

She goes into full scold now, with the wagging finger and everything. "That is just sad and pathetic, that you have to hide behind jokes instead of allowing yourself to really feel."

I can only guess from her response to the literature that Dad has slipped some more recent, more serious offerings in there among the goofy rhymes he made up for us when we were three, and seven, and ten, and twelve, and fifteen.

"Sorry, Molly. Didn't mean to be hiding." Except that I did. "Emotion and feelings and stuff can be hard, y'know?"

She points at me, and smiles a smile of one who truly believes she has the answer to the question.

"You should come to church with me, Kiki. It helps, it really does, to unlock a person, and open them up to . . ."

She trails off when she sees my own smile and, I suppose, my jackass back-of-class body language.

"Did I say something funny?" she says, grim as God.

"Well . . . yeah, come on, Molly. Jesus saves? Please. Jesus, just save it, is what I feel like telling him. You believe all that stuff, do you? You feel as if you are *saved*, yes? Got yourself all sorted out, have you?"

There is nothing cute about her great big eyes narrowed at me right now.

"Are those my clothes?" she asks without gesture.

"Yup," I say too brightly. "Here you go, ma'am."

She comes up to take her clean clothes out of my hands. I hang on to them tightly. As if we are playing. She tries for a couple of seconds to tug them away but then refuses to play.

"At least Jesus isn't an asshole," she says.

"Well, the jury is still out on—"

"Shut *up*," she snaps. "Just because you are proud to be emotionally retarded, that does not give you the right to trash my beliefs."

"I prefer, 'emotionally subnormal.'"

"Shut *up*. No, I am not all sorted out. I know that. But

yes, I do feel saved, and I do get something from the communion of souls, and the beautiful and positive and healing messages of the church, and the forgiveness that is always there if I have honest sorrow for the things I've done. And if my church, my community, my belief system does that for me, why should the likes of *you* think you have a better idea when it is so obvious you don't have any idea at all? Mockery and criticism of everybody else is a shit religion, Kiki."

God. And I mean that sincerely.

I blink forty times before speaking, just to get some moisture back in my eyes after Molly's sandblasting.

"I was out of line," I say quietly. "I really am sorry. Forgive me?"

Now she snatches the clothes away from me. "Of course I forgive you. That's what we do," she says, with the old smile and bright big eyes back in place. "But now I have to go to confession for all that scolding I just did. Thanks, jerk."

"Sorry. Hey, that sorry thing gets easier the more you do it."

"But you have to mean it or it doesn't . . . Wow, you folded these. And"—she sniffs—"fabric softener."

"See," I say, "how's that for a real man. Pretty butch, or what?"

She spins back in the direction of my room. "I don't know if I'd call it butch, but it's not half bad, either. Still, you could learn a lot about expressing yourself from your father." She slams the door on that one.

Oh, yes, back where we started, the poetry. Why do all roads lead back to that man?

"Okay, I have to go," Molly says, sweeping back into view, sniffing the sleeve of her freshly laundered blouse as she does. Her hair, after the shower and good long sleep, looks precisely as it did before, and precisely as it has every time I've seen her. Browns-helmet perfect, Browns-helmet tough.

Even her hair is resilient.

"How come you have to go?" I ask, and before I can even register, she has marched right on up and into me and is squeezing me hard around my waist and reflexively I am squeezing back, hugging her close to me and it feels lovely beyond what words could ever convey. Take that, poetry.

"Stacey and I have work chores at the hostel. Cleaning and stuff. Pays our way. Can't say no when they ask. Sometimes they send us out to other places that need us, but today we're just staying home. I'll never get it as clean as this place, though, that's for sure."

She hugs me quietly for a bit more. I absorb it, with every available nerve ending, for several silent seconds.

"Thanks for being uncommon," says the broken mold herself.

"See, didn't I tell you I wasn't like those other guys?"

"No, you're just like them. But you're uncommon for at least trying not to be."

Cover blown. Do I hate being seen, being known like that? Do I love it?

"Could I walk with you?" I say. "To the hostel?"

"Sure you can," she says, stepping back and hooking my broken arm with her probably formerly broken one.

It stinks like she's been hoarding shrimp tails and chicken bones in there.

Stacey is at the top of the creaky wooden steps that lead to the front door of the old Victorian that is now the St. Cecelia Youth Hostel. Stacey doesn't look saintly or even youthful but does look like a mean hostile old lady as we ascend the stairs toward her. Feels like a lot of stairs.

"Did you ball my innocent and trusting young friend, you wicked thing?"

I am about to protest the language at least, when Molly turns to me, asking loudly, "Is she talking to you, or me?"

Not that it changes the honest answer in either case, though if it's me, I plan to make a little ambiguity go a long way in a good cause.

No matter, since Mother Stacey is grinning at us by the time we reach her anyway.

"I see," she says, poking me in the ribs with a finger like

a hockey stick that almost sends me tumbling backward whence I came. "The old, would-you-like-to-come-up-to-my-place-and-see-my-father's-book-of-poetry ploy, eh? Had a lot of success with that one have ya, studley?"

"A one-hundred-percent success rate so far, now that you ask."

"Ahh, that's sweet." She pokes me again, and it's even harder.

She can poke me all she wants, because nothing that's happened today is doing anything to lessen the whole experience for me. I feel like I'm living, here, with these two, reputation enhancement or not. Living more than I did in the past, and I'm loving it and too grateful to tell them.

But I am starting to wonder if Stacey is seriously displeased, or playing, or some of both, and why? Not that I could ever say it, but with Molly's track record, what do I matter, in the overall scheme of things?

"Well, we've got sins to scrub away," Stacey says, pulling Molly under a big protective paw and hauling her inside.

"See ya later, Kiki," Molly calls over her shoulder, a sort of wrestle going on just for her to get an angle to wave back at me properly. "It was really wonderful. You were really wonderful."

"Oh jeez, stop it already," Stacey barks at her.

She is clearly getting all kinds of wrong impression there.

I just might have the beginnings of a reputation, a life, *and* a tribe that will let me be an insider.

For my next trick, I'm thinking I may walk on my hands all the way back, to my home, from theirs.

WHERE THEY DON'T HAVE TO TAKE YOU IN, BUT THEY DO

Maybe there was a reasonable explanation," Jasper said as he led me down the abandoned train tracks again. We were not walking back to school, just walking to walk, leaving Michelle the Renter on the steps waiting for the Homeowner. And walk we did. The six miles *almost* to the school, and then turning, without break, in the direction of home again.

His home, that was. Because he had one.

"The explanation is, he's a selfish, cowardly bastard," I said. We had just made the pivot point onto the return leg. My phone rang, again. There were only two people who would be likely to call me, and one of them was right beside me, urging me to answer.

"Perhaps, if you hear what he has to say, the answer might have a little more complexity to it than that."

"Whose side are you on here, Jasper?"

"Side? Jesus, Kiki, does everything have to be like that? You have a gift for seeing these imaginary forces always aligned against you. Of course I am on your side. But can't I be *for* you without being *against* your father?"

I was walking at a good clip now, breaking a sweat. He was keeping up but hanging a couple of steps behind as we talked. Probably trying to unsettle me.

"No!" I said, with the ringtone as accompaniment. "And don't call me Kiki."

"Grrr," he said. "Grr. Right, right, you know what you are? I just realized, you know what you are?"

"I'm pretty sure nothing that started with that question has ever ended well, so I'm just going to not answer."

It was a pretty flawed blocking strategy.

"You are like an opposite Walter Mitty character. You're an inverse Walter Mitty, is what you are. You know the character, Walter Mitty, who fantasizes his way into all kinds of fantastic situations where life is exciting and he is the star?"

I did not have to entertain him if I chose not to.

"Never met the man," I said, walking just a bit faster.

"Doesn't matter. You are the inverse, because you spend your time constantly imagining that everything is terrible and everyone is conspiring wickedness and you are the victim. You are the Walter Mitty of self-pity."

Sometimes you hear something and immediately recognize it as something evil that needs instant extinguishing.

"Hey," he said, all chipper all of a sudden. "Did you hear that? The Walter Mitty of self-pity. Oh, that has wheels, that one. Don't you—"

"No!" I snapped because I very well heard it and did not love the thought of hearing it for the rest of my life. "Just go back to calling me Kiki, that'll be fine."

He was laughing robustly when my phone rang again. He didn't tell me to answer it this time. Instead, he scooted right up behind me and snagged the thing right out of my pants pocket.

"Hey!" I shouted as he raced past me and up the tracks.

"Hello," he said, running hard to stay just out of my reach. "Yes, sir. Jasper. His friend. Yup, I'm the one."

"Give me that," I said, grabbing the phone and giving the side of his head a well-earned smack at the same time. Jasper stopped running and started laughing as I addressed the caller.

"So, your new roommate is all moved in now, I guess. Excellent. Have a good summer, and stop calling me." I hung up on him.

Jasper and I resumed walking, but at a more reasonable talking pace.

"He's trying to discuss it with you," he said.

"I don't want to hear it."

"That's stupid."

"I don't care what you think."

"Well, ah, yes you do. More likely, you are afraid to hear him out because he might say something perfectly reasonable and then that'll blow the *Good Ship Boo-fucking-hoo* right out of the water. Then where will you be?"

I couldn't be sure but I was getting the impression Jasper had the stamina to keep up with this indefinitely. I knew I couldn't.

It was already exhausting me. *I* was exhausting me.

"Okay, okay, okay," I said, stopping and grabbing him desperately by the collar. "You might have some points in there somewhere. Maybe. But you know, Jasper, it's been a pretty shit couple of years, parents breaking up—twice. Coming to live with my dad, feeling like this was going to be an awesome new turn in both of our lives until he welcomes me as if I had come to audit his taxes for the last ten years. I haven't been able to get my feet under me for long enough to believe I'm not a total cripple, and the only person I have been able to make any real contact with at all is you. And you're an asshole."

I felt like I had already kind of tested my limits there with Mr. Jasper as he stood silently, looking me in the eyes. Then he looked at my hands still clutching his shirt.

"This actually makes you seem almost kinda manly, this thing you're doing with the grabbing."

"Sorry, man," I said, letting go and for some reason brushing my hands off quickly on my own shirt. "I just can't talk to him today, all right? I'm way too angry to even listen to him. I mean, whatever he has to say, it doesn't change the reality that that woman takes over our house—sorry, *his* house since obviously I don't own squat—next week! And I didn't know anything about it until *she* told me."

"Fair enough, fair enough," he said, first holding up his hands like he was stopping traffic, then patting me on the chest warmly with them. "So, let me ask, would you say yes to dinner at my house this time?"

I actually focus for a couple seconds, on the sensation caused by his simply putting his hands flat on my chest. Nice. Human contact, even small measures, was a very welcome something I had been missing.

"If you didn't invite me, I was just going to invite myself."

As we walked up the stairs to Jasper's second-floor apartment, I remembered my remark about Dad's house and how I didn't own anything. I regretted my tone, and my presumption that owning property was just a happy natural something, like beards or breasts, that would eventually come to everybody.

"Is your mother not here?" I asked as I sat at his tidy pine kitchen table. It had three matching chairs, with the fourth side pushed up to a wall.

"Nah, Ma works these hours usually. She's a cook, so that means most nights around now she's cooking a lot of other folks their dinner while I am cooking my own. Sort of like we're cooking together, only separately. On her off nights, though, we cook together, only together."

It got to me, that last bit. "That's, pretty great, Jasper, the way you guys work."

He was systematically assembling items on the counter by the stove in preparation for his cooking. "Yeah. We're cool, Ma and me."

I knew it was just the two of them living here, but I hadn't asked about any other parties and possible whereabouts. Now, though, there didn't seem to be any pieces missing.

Naturally, I wanted to blurt out how I was jealous and he was lucky, and how I didn't have anybody like that anywhere in my life. But I had learned at least enough to know that if I did any bellyaching now, I'd be doing it on an empty stomach and out on the street.

Which would have been bad. My stomach, come to think of it, was looking forward to dinner.

Jasper went at it like a professional diner chef. He flipped on a radio, which sat on a shelf above the stove, nestled in with all the little cylinders of spices. Classic rock played over his head and wafted my way while he threw ingredients at a big, snapping, popping, oily skillet. It was a heavy metal pan, that skillet, and could swiftly make a pancake out of any unruly diner.

"Get back, or I will surely bash you," he said when I ventured innocently toward his handiwork. "You'll see it when it's ready, which will be a couple more minutes. Till then you'll just have to sit there and make do with the scent."

The scent would just about do all by itself.

A song by the Supremes started up. Immediately, I was taken somewhere else as I recognized it as a personal favorite of my mother's. She had very few favorites, as she was no great lover of music, so this was something. "The Happening," that was the name of the song. It was a good choice for a person who was only going to have a few favorites. Made me bob my head in time.

I scanned the room, just killing time. There wasn't much room to scan anyway, and the wall right next to me on the table's fourth side had a big framed picture of Jesus flashing his Sacred Heart down on everybody. I thought he was supposed to be more modest than that.

He was useful, though, just to fill out a foursome if Jasper and his mother and I were playing pinochle or bridge or something. He obviously couldn't play, but he'd look good filling the space, like those people they hire to cover for stars when they go to the bathroom during the Academy Awards show.

I was thinking about Jesus and his heart filling one of those toilet seats at the Oscars when my phone blipped its text message signal. The Lord's distraction must have caused me to open the message from Dad.

I was afraid to tell you the plans. I was wrong.

It could have been three hours I stared at that message but I only became aware of time again when Jasper slapped two big aromatic plates down on the table.

"Oh," I said, startled. Anyone would have been. "Did you just make all this? Just now?"

He deposited the food, cutlery, condiments, and napkins on the table and then went back to the fridge. "No, I phoned for takeout and had it delivered. What did you think I was doing over there all that time?"

"Well, cooking, of course," I said. "But I meant, specifically, this, did you *make* this, like from the ground up as opposed to heating ready-made?" I bent low to inhale the vapors off what looked like the finest hash I had ever encountered. There was an extra-large poached egg settled bull's-eye in the middle of it all, with barbecued beans and chunky buttered cornbread on the sides.

"I guess that's your version of a compliment to the chef, so thanks. Yes, I did every bit of it. Okay, not the cornbread. Ma gets to tuck away bits and pieces from work, off cuts of meat, produce that's approaching sell-by, the kind of thing that isn't of use to them but that makes dynamite casserole/ hash/stir-fry kind of deals around here. Oh, and stale cornbread, which fries up spectacularly."

"Outrageous," I said, talking through my food like a barbarian. The classic rock guys were sending us rockabilly something now, which was thoughtful.

"Good, then Chef is pleased," he said as he took the seat opposite me. He plunked down a big bottle of Coke and two pint glasses half filled with ice. Then, he started pouring from the main attraction.

"What is that?" I asked when he had unloaded golden-brown something into each glass.

"My mother's dark rum," he said, topping both glasses off with the Coke. He passed one over to me.

"Should you be taking it?" I asked.

He extended his glass across the table where it was met by mine and we achieved clink.

"It was a gift from her boss, who got it as a gift himself. But he hates the stuff. Then she brought it home. We tried it the other night and lucky us, she hates it too. She told me it was all mine . . . but I suppose you can have a little."

"Lucky us," I said.

"A toast to the end of the school year," he said, reclinking before drinking.

"And the beginning of summer," I said with a bit of a sneer.

He frowned at me, but drank deeply.

I drank, maybe a little less deeply, but enough to draw a conclusion.

"Who in the world could not love this?" I said, looking at the glass like the answer was readable there. The rich heavy rum went right down into my stomach and spread out to warm all areas of my torso. I hadn't done a great deal of drinking up to that point, but enough to know when something nice agreed with me and this was that something nice. Certainly something like a miracle was at work that could get the loveliness down into my belly *and* all up and tingly under my scalp at the same time.

"Glad you like it," he said. "Don't let your food get cold. I wouldn't want to see what all those scraps looked like if they congealed and tried to re-form into what they once were."

"Ha!" I said, finding the funny to way outweigh the queasy in that sequence. I applied myself to the task of conspicuous consumption, savoring every bite of every bit.

And every sip and every slug.

"I know," Jasper said even though I was pretty sure I hadn't said anything for him to agree with.

"I know," I said in turn to the glow-chested dinner companion levitating on my right. Jasper was leaning over and topping up my drink, which was approximately number three. It would have been tough to get a precise read on that because he was just alternating top-ups now, rather than mixing every time. A rum, then a Coke, then next time a rum again. They were practically the same color, so no matter.

Ping. Text message.

"Whoa, somebody's suddenly popular," he said as I retrieved it.

Truth is summer planned long ago before you came. Vy complicated. Teaching. Peru. Brilliant opportunity. Thought you would go back to Mom anyway. We should talk.

"Uh-oh," Jasper said, looking at my face.

I handed him my phone, and went immediately back to the last few bites of my meal. Then I put down my fork and sat back, patting my belly with both hands like you're supposed to at such moments.

"Best meal I ever had, in my whole life, Jasper my friend. I cannot thank you enough."

From our opposite sides, we both made the same move, lurching across the table, as he handed back my phone and I collected my drink.

"That's not so great, huh?" he said, pointing at my phone as if that were necessary.

I took a big gulp, and he joined in solidarity.

"No, on the contrary," I responded, looking at the phone

in my hand, "I've found it to be an excellent phone."

There was a pause, then a dawning, then the two of us burst out in a huge, post-meal, tension-breaking laugh that made us sound like a whole barroom and diner all by ourselves. We got up then and started tidying up together with some grandstanding rock opera thing coming out of the radio and into us.

He let me wash the dishes while he cleaned and straightened. And poured. The music was generous, not even pausing when Jasper reached up to the shelf with one hand to return the pepper grinder and the other hand to turn up the volume and only managed to drop both items clattering down on the stove top. We laughed at that one for about an hour.

We talked, too, as the rum ran down and so did I. But that combination of factors was making comprehension and recall kind of like juggling three bowling pins when you can really only manage tennis balls. We talked about fathers. Turned out he did have one, but the rest of the story got away somewhere. Talked about the superior fathers we would be eventually. I remembered that, all of that, although the radio or the refrigerator could probably be superior to the fathers we had.

We never even left the kitchen, which surely is the sign of a successful dinner party.

My knees felt a little watery as I finished the washing and

backed away from the sink. My everything felt a little watery, I noticed.

"Thanks, so so much for everything, Jasper," I said as I sloshed in the general direction of the door.

"It's gonna turn out all right," he said.

I turned around before getting through the kitchen doorway, and when I did, he was right there.

"What?" I said.

"Your Dad stuff. I know it looks shitty, but I still believe it'll straighten out."

I heard my breath then, huff-puffing so fast through my nostrils, I almost believed it wasn't me but the old train line that had suddenly come back to life just up the road.

"I'm so angry, Jasper," I said.

"I understand how you feel, and you have every right," he said. Then he did that warm-hands thing again on my chest.

"I don't want to go back there," I said.

"I wasn't going to let you," he said.

SENSE OF PURPOSE

You'd almost think I had places to be, things to do, by the bop in my walk now.

My world is taking on something of a shape with the people I've met and the places I am finding. I know I need to go farther and figure out next moves and next moves beyond those, but right now what I've fallen into for a life doesn't have me in a rush to climb back out again.

"Ah, there you are, man," Mickey says, giving me a hearty running-for-office handshake. It's raining lightly, the sand is even more like dirt than usual, and Mickey's wearing an oil-stained tan trenchcoat that would not be out of place in a spy movie from the 1930s, which is when the thing was last dry-cleaned. "Why aren't we seeing more of you, Kikidiki?"

"I don't know," I say, trying to look past him and all around without being too obvious about it.

"The girls ain't here, man. Nobody hangs around this depressing mud pit when it rains unless they got no options whatsoever. And girls, dude, girls *always* have options, know what I'm sayin'?" He laughs a hoarse and stoney laugh. "Lucky bitches, right?"

"Right, I guess," I say.

Behind Mickey, his pals Tailbone and Howard have somehow commandeered a half-deflated rubber life raft and are huddled under it, smoking. Much of the smoke seems to be rolling up and getting stuck under the raft bottom by their heads and making what seems to be their own private noxious microclimate.

"Sorry, brother," Mickey says to me while gesturing toward them. "You want to come in out of the rain? It's not much, but our shelter and bounty are yours to share."

I crouch down to try to get a glimpse of the guys' raft-and-smoke-obscured faces. It's out of morbid curiosity more than any real intention of joining them.

"Hi, guys," I say.

They both wave. I straighten back up.

"I appreciate the offer," I say to Mickey. "But I think I'll just continue on my way, see if I can catch up with the girls somewhere."

"Sure, sure. Wouldn't expect them to show here anytime today. They were here yesterday, though. Both of 'em. Not together, though. First time I saw that big one—"

"Stacey."

"Yeah, first time I saw Stacey on her own, and man, I was goin' for it. I was practically goin' pogo all the way up the beach to get to her, if you know what I'm sayin', but then she just done like a scared rabbit and shot off before I got even close. I'm bettin' there's lots o' bunny in that gal and I'm aimin' to—"

"Yeah, Mickey, right. What about Molly? She came by herself as well?"

"No, dude, she had a dude. Seen him another time too, which is like, a *relationship* right there. They was here once before, and then twice yesterday, so that's like, wedding bells and shit. Guy must be a priest or a bishop or somethin' to get into impressin' Good Golly Molly to that degree. Looked like a priest, actually, now that I think about it. Anyway, chicks ain't everything. Don't run off so fast, we want you to hang out."

"Another time," I say, running now up the mucky beach.

Crystal City is a grim place when it rains. Stray dogs in clumpy, matted pairs and threes seem to populate every vacant lot, both the lots and the mutts seemingly brought to life if you just add water. The streets are paved with the cheap-grade tarmac that causes car tires to make maddening, incessant sluck sounds as they roll by. Heat sticks to everything and seems to increase with the rain rather than there being any cooling benefit at all.

Yesterday, bright and blue and balmy, I didn't go to the beach when even Crystal Beach must have shined. Yesterday was my neighborhood day, my quiet, slow, drift day, which worked a treat and was just the right thing at just the right time. I went for a good long swim in the municipal pool, which is sadly underused but not sad for me personally. Waters speak words when they're allowed, and it was a fine fifty, chatty, reassuring lengths of the pool. It also told me that I'm out of shape, but was kind about it.

I had lunch in one of Syd's locals and received every ounce of hospitality he surely would have gotten if he were there himself. I received a serving of a spinach and feta cheese pie called spanakopita that was gold-medal gourmet, probably intended to serve a whole family and costing less than I would normally pay for a hot dog. There was a side dish of a grated pickled carrot-beet-parsnip medley that in a stroke overturned my relationship to root vegetables for life.

And after that I slouched across the street to the public library, where sticky closed windows and summer swelter and chunky old dark gumwood everywhere created the perfect conditions for lazy digestion of foods and words.

The poetry section, abandoned to me alone. I had to. I scanned quickly for my selections and bundled the team up with me in the fat leather chair that was heroically reproducing the sweat of a century of sensitive word-nerds who had sat there before me.

It took the entire afternoon. But I had an entire afternoon to give it.

I wasn't wrong. My memory had not convulsed to the point of jolting poetic language entirely out of my ken. The Edgar Allan Poe and Seamus Heaney and Edna St. Vincent Millay and Dylan Thomas that I learned to love in another time were still in there with me when I wanted them. When I called them, when I needed to.

I could still read the poets without having to become one.

It was a great and empowering day by any measure.

But I should have gone to the beach. Because it was a beach day, and beach days should be Kiki days.

And because if I went to the beach, I would not have bumbled into the library's media room as I tried to leave.

"Can just anybody use these?" I asked the librarian dusting the keyboards and screens of the three wide-open computers in the glass-walled, temperature-controlled, bedroom-size space.

"No," she said, itching my nose with a smile and a feather duster, "but you can."

She left the room then and returned to her quiet, untroubled front desk of summertime.

Leaving me alone with the computers. I reminded myself that I owned a perfectly wonderful, new and shiny and indestructible laptop that I deliberately left at home, along with my phone, in order to get away for real and for good. No messy ties. No looking backward.

And that was good, so, well done me. Something to prove, and I proved it.

Therefore, I had done the hard part and had earned at least a glance at my e-mail.

I had to admit that as I sat down and called it up, I was feeling like a little kid who had to run away *loudly* and keep checking over his shoulder to be sure that people noticed and the "please don't go" pleading could begin.

I opened my e-mail, and there they were.

Both of them.

Jasper had e-mailed me twice. Once, the day I left.

J: *Are you all right? That's all I want to know. Actually, I want to know a shitload more than that. But, are you all right?*

Then, the next day.

J: *How could you run off, on the very day you finally became an insider?*

At that instant I became horrifyingly aware of being in a glass room in the middle of a public building. I swiveled around in my chair so hard in my self-defeating desperation to seem casual that I did nearly a complete three-sixty before stopping myself again. This caught the eye of the librarian, the only other person in the place. I waved too happily when she looked too concerned.

Back to the computer, and the climate control did me no good now. I started to sweat, at the hairline and back of the neck, and I got a bit of the shakes like I was right there and then in the middle of some crazed and dangerously taboo activity.

I was right in thinking I needed to be out of Jasper's orbit just now. I could freak myself out just fine without his working at it.

Dad also wrote that first day.

D: *I am petrified and mortified and owe you a lot of things, but first I just need to hear from you so I can stop worrying about you.*

Huh. Worried about me, was he? Well, what do you know? Shame. He'll probably get over it.

When he did not hear back from me, he started getting in touch on a surprisingly regular basis. Again, huh, imagine that.

D: *Please?*

And thank you.

D: *I know that you are out there. I know that you can hear me.*

Was he building bridges here, or preparing to chase me through the woods with a meat cleaver?

D: *Son? I have done everything wrong. I realize that now. Son?*

Not fair. Jeez. He shouldn't have called me that. There should be rules. He should be able to lose the right until earning it back, like stripes in the army.

And it shouldn't have worked on me, either. It shouldn't have given me butterflies, that was just pathetic.

Did the man have a lot of time for me all of a sudden, now that I was gone?

I shut down the computer, keeping my thoughts for myself, and left the library.

ALL KINDS OF TIRED

I ring the bell and I knock on the door and I ring the bell and I knock on the door until I am guaranteed to be either answered or arrested.

I feel like I have achieved both, when Stacey comes to the door.

"What are you doing, knucklehead?" she says, exasperated.

"I'm coming calling, what do you think? Where you guys been? Come on out to play." And this is where I get all slick and cool. "Where's Molly, anyway?"

"We've been working, actually," she says, and looks tired enough that it's probably true. "And because we don't have an *uncle* looking out for us, with his steaks and his glistening porcelain and his amazing soft bathrobes and whatever all else for luxuries, we have to work consistently if we want to sleep under a roof consistently."

"C'mon, Stacey. What's going on? What's the matter? All I want is to see you guys. What's wrong with that? We're a tribe, right? Let's just be a tribe. . . . Let's just go someplace—"

"No!" she snaps. "I am someplace. I mean, it's no place but it's someplace and I need to be here. Most people don't have the kind of freedom you seem to have."

This is the first time I have witnessed such a short fuse on Stacey. It is a sad sight in the shadow of her more rollicking regular self.

"Right," I say. "We should probably talk another time. You're obviously having a bad day."

"They're *all* bad, you fool. I have no home. I'm in here scrubbing toilets and pulling three-foot-long snakes of human hair and mucus and eel jelly out of drains because the goodly folks in charge keep reminding me I'll be out on my ear if I don't. *And* for the comedy kicker, I'm forced to go to church every morning to pray and thank *Him* for the privilege and good fortune of it all."

It's the kind of thing you can't really respond to, even if you have a response. Which, I don't.

"Sorry about all that, Stacey. But, maybe Molly—"

"She's not here, Kiki, all right? She's not here, and she's not going to be here. She stayed out again, and she lost her place and that was that, but she doesn't care, because she's living with Billy now, so she wasn't bothered about that at all. Right? You get it? She thinks that this Billy is just the big everything and so good luck to her and God bless her and whatever. People never stay in these places for very long anyway and in fact I'm not long for this one myself now."

"What? No, it's too soon. Don't leave already. I only just met you."

She looks about to growl at me but then her face muscles shift a little and soften and I think she feels somewhat sorry for me, which is fine, which will do just fine.

"I have to get back to work, Kiki, or these people are gonna make the decision for me."

"Okay, okay, then you should go. Will I see you later?"

She shrugs. "Maybe. I don't know. Right now I'm just . . . tired. All kinds of tired."

"What about Molly?"

She shrugs again. "What about her? She's gonna do what she's gonna do."

"But . . . but, I thought . . ."

"Don't think that."

"But, no. You don't understand. It was special. It was different. She was—"

"She has been looking for you, though," Stacey says, the

nicest words coming through a hard-knuckle delivery that feels like a backhander dope slap.

"What? See? Why didn't you tell me that?"

"Because what she wants is to borrow your book. Your father's poetry. I wasn't sure you'd find that the most pleasant development."

"My father's book?" I say weakly.

"She wants to show it to Billy. Soulful-sensitive type, apparently, though if you asked me, I'd say when he looks in a mirror there's nobody looking back, but what do I know. So I guess she wants to read to him, from your dad's poetry. And maybe he'll read some to her, too. Fucking sweet, huh?"

I guess Dad's collection ranges a fair bit beyond his classic, "Could Kevin from Heaven/Really be Seven?"

Stacey's eyes are going cold-stare as she speaks, and her voice is losing power.

"You being deliberately nasty to me, Stacey?"

"Yes, I am. Because I can't be bothered to work up the energy to support your fantasy life at the moment. Rich boy goes slumming, sweeps troubled street chick off her feet, blah blah blah. And your naïveté is getting tedious so I'm trying to help you get through it quicker and get to your fucking manhood already so I can get back to, you know, life the real thing."

I am physically recoiling from her, backing down the

stairs. She keeps looking at me as I do and I think I see the softening again, the better thing inside her, and some regret for the unkindness. I know that is in there, in her.

And yet. How the hell would I know that?

"Rich?" I say with pleading hands as I look up at her from the sidewalk. "I got nothing, just like you. I am just like you."

Her response is an almighty slam of the door.

FUNNY THING

I always thought libraries were merely books. And, maybe, free passes to the science museum.

And I always thought they were just dotted, here, maybe there, and okay one more there. The way chunks of dough are distributed in low-price cookie-dough ice cream just enough to be legitimate but not enough to make you really *believe.*

That was when I lived in other places, though. In other *people's* places.

Now, since I am living in a Crystal place that feels mine, in a life that feels mine, where nobody is overseeing me and I have to notice for myself . . . well, it's changed.

Libraries pop up where you need them. They magically materialize at just the point where you think, *This neighborhood could use a . . .*

I suppose they were possibly there all along. Maybe I

failed to notice, when I didn't need to notice.

Now I notice. It's no more than a block away from Stacey's hostel, on the very route I walked to get there, and it did not show itself before.

"Are those computers for anybody to use?" I ask the solitary librarian.

"No," she says, "not just anybody . . ."

I don't even care who trained them to say that, or if they were in a huge auditorium with six hundred librarians repeating after him, "not just anybody . . ." I will look forward to hearing that in every library everywhere from now on.

I log on.

J: *You did nothing wrong. No matter what you are thinking, you did nothing wrong.*

Please come home.

Nice finish. You would think that the stupid, childish, pathetic welling up and welling over that my eyes are doing would be triggered by the words "Please come home," written by my friend when until recently I did not have one actual friend to my knowledge. But no, it's even stupider and more childish and more pathetic because I started losing it back at "you did nothing wrong."

And then there's the other one.

D: *I canceled it. Canceled it all. Made a great, glorious*

mess, is what I did. A whole country, Peru, is mad at me, and it appears I am facing legal action of some kind from Michelle whose plans I have ruined, but I damn well dammit did it.

Funny thing. In some uncomfortable ways—financial, professional, social, etc.—this feels like the mayhem of breakdowns past.

But this time I don't feel bad. This time I feel like I did the better thing, consequences be damned.

I'm in my chair now, son. Settled and waiting for you to come back.

Like I should have been doing all along. Like I will continue to do.

Please come home.

My face is buried in my hands as I sense the librarian inch up next to me, professional-close but not weirdo close, and I feel like screaming out for her to get away from me but I am also screaming *in* to please, please don't go away.

When did these places become so complicated?

TRIBAL

The rain is merely mist when I join the guys again on the beach. They are sitting inside the raft now, and the three of them raise a big cheer as I approach them.

"Well, allll riiiiight!" Mickey whoops.

"Yeah," yelps Howard.

"Whoa ho," shouts Tailbone.

Now, this is more like it. It feels nice to be appreciated. Even though they might be stoned enough to think I'm somebody else.

Killing time here on Crystal Beach is not something you have to do, because it basically seems to kill itself. Time suicide. That sounds like a bad thing but it's not. In fact, it's a compliment. You slip into it, this Crystal reality, this pace that works for people with nowhere really to go. And before you have really clocked what's happening, not only have many hours chewed themselves right off the clock, but the beach itself has evolved and improved, till it's the equal of anybody else's beach, and you are damned well ready to fight to defend its honor.

People who at first glance you were snorting at become people whose company you now value.

All manner of folk suddenly make sense. There are all manner of tribes outside and beyond the ones I had always known and failed to fit. I won't always fail to fit, I know that now.

"I wouldn't ever want to live in a house again," Tailbone says as he passes me the wine. I simply cannot stand up to as much smoke as these guys do, so eventually I volunteered to spring for a few bottles if one of the legal-age guys would go and get it. Howard is the oldest, at twenty-three, but more important he has the grizzled thing from when he was in the army, and the oft-broken nose and fingers and leathery outdoors face. He has a liquor store face, and is probably always the guy who does the run.

"Why not?" I ask. I feel now like I really want to know these things, about this life. I haven't even done anything wrong, and Stacey's made me feel ashamed and exposed and like I need to retake and pass an important test on the subject.

"Because all the time I lived in a house, with my ma and dad and all those little shit brothers and sisters, then later with my roommates, then, prison, I realized that all those years, all of them, I was always so tense, always like, crazed with the tension. And that was what made me mental, is what I think. Made me do all them things I shouldn'ta wanted to do. And from what all I saw of the people I was locked in with, in all those places, they all had exactly the same problem that was doggin' me. Every single person I ever lived with acted in a way that made me want to shoot 'em right in the head. Everybody feels that way, for sure. Tension, man, tension everywhere."

"And this," I say, "comes down to being indoors?"

"Exactly," Tailbone says excitedly. "Exactly, exactly. You said that so well, Kiki man. Wow, it's so great to have a intellectual guy hangin' with us, isn't it, guys?"

"Yeah," Howard says, raising one of the other wine bottles.

"Yeah," Mickey says, on his knees tending our modest, discreet campfire.

The weather cleared for a while and then veered back in the direction of wet and uncomfortable as the night got deep. It's made it difficult to keep a decent flame going, but it's also kept the numbers down here on the beach, so that is a fair exchange in my mind.

I have never seen the beach this quiet. Even with us yammering away, the modest sound of the surf slurp is with us all the time.

"I even like the rain," Tailbone says.

"I do too," I say, then I tip the wine bottle way back and gulp big, to murmurs of support from my crew.

"Frisbee," Mickey says out of nowhere, and everyone responds by jumping up.

Oh. Well. Maybe jumping is a bit ambitious right now. My legs do a wobble and I am almost down crosslegged in the dirty mud-sand again. But I catch myself, give my head a strong doggy-at-the-beach shake, and I am ready to join the guys for Frisbee.

The guys who, by the way, suffered none of my shakiness despite having pounded themselves with at least three times as much of anything as I did. I find myself aspiring to their hardcoreness, even as the thought unsettles me, and my stomach.

I give myself a full-body doggy shake as I get in the Frisbee rotation.

"I think we should get a dog," I say as I catch my first throw. I drop it, of course, pick it up, and pass to Howard.

"Awesome idea," Howard says, passing on to Mickey.

"That is a lot of responsibility," Mickey-the-Dad says, passing to Tailbone.

"Dogs suck," says Tailbone, passing sharply to me.

"Listen," Mickey says serenely, "we'll think about it, Kiki, okay. I can't make any promises, but we'll consider maybe getting ourselves a dog at some point."

"But we already have *Howard*," Tailbone shouts.

Howard takes off on what probably feels like a ferocious bull charge to him but looks from the outside like a lanky penguin running with his head down. He barely grazes Tailbone, goes tumbling right past him and down into the sand. Then Tailbone drops down on top of him. A form of wrestling ensues.

"C'mon," Mickey says, tugging me by the shirt to walk with him down to the water's edge.

The rain is refusing to be ignored now. But it's still somehow not hard to live with it, despite the fact my previous feeling about any precipitation was that it was a curse sent down to smite me personally for whatever transgressions I had committed. This evening I feel like I'm sharing it, and that it's a benign presence.

"Do you skip rocks?" Mickey says.

It is mostly dark now. There is enough light left that you could see the crests of waves or the ticks of a good flat rock across the surface of an otherwise invisible sea. But mostly, visibility really isn't much.

"Is that some kind of freaky code you're speaking now, Mick?" I ask with high comic seriousness.

He pauses the pause of a smart guy on dope.

"I wasn't," he says thoughtfully. "But that's pretty good. It's funny, right. And it fits, too. Which is why it's good. Nice work."

"Thanks. I try."

"But if you wanna speak that code, we could do that, too."

Oh. A seriously inadvertent turn there. Jeez, now what have I done?

"Are you saying what I think you're saying?" I say.

He is crouched down, there in the dark sand under the dark sky, raking around for flat rocks, presumably.

"I don't know. Depends what you think I'm saying. What do you think I'm saying? Maybe you should just say it."

"Ah, that's what you would *like* me to do, isn't it? I'm falling right into your trap. You get your jollies making me say what it is I think you're saying. Then, you practically don't even have to say it because I've done it all for you."

Mickey looks up at me, with a clutch of rocks in one hand as he balances his crouch with the other. "Is this another code? 'Cause I think I fell behind here."

I extend my hand to give him a lift up, even though I'm not exactly the rock of steadiness myself.

"Nah, man. I was just saying that yes, I used to skip rocks like a champion, but haven't in a long time. And right now my equilibrium is in a state where, it's not the best time to try again."

He seems—then I realize, pretends—to be working hard to decipher my words.

"Right, so you used to skip. But you don't anymore."

"Correct."

"Funny, I'm the opposite. I never used to skip. I was dead against that shit, man. Then, gradually, when I was living on the streets I became more . . . universal. Call it the enlightenment of deprivation maybe, but I decided after a while that if somebody wants to love you, let 'em. Today, I skip all the time."

I do wish I could see his expression as he approaches the water to sling his first stone.

"This time you were definitely speaking code, right?" I say.

"Yes, sir, I was," he says, and I hear his first throw plunk into the water without a single skip.

This seems like a good point to throw rocks and not talk.

There is probably a point beyond which rain doesn't matter, has no more effect on the human body, but for whatever reasons, Mickey, Howard, Tailbone, and myself are still on the beach way past when any sense, common or otherwise, would tell you to go home.

Of course, I know, go *home* is not an option for any of them.

But go *somewhere* certainly is.

The four of us are sitting under the lifeboat, which is once again upturned. Up and down our little line a joint is passing, along with a cigarette and the remains of one bottle of red wine and one bottle of rosé. We are all pointed in the direction of the ocean, though with the darkness and lateness and weather heaviness and eye blurriness we could just as well be facing into the back of a garage except for the fact it is the ocean, and for the fact that we know.

"You know where you're going to go, tonight, to sleep?" I ask.

"Oh, yeah," they all say in their own distinctive ways of saying the same thing no matter how many times they say it. Nobody, however, adds any detail to that answer.

They don't even ask me. By now I reek of it, what Stacey said about me and my being all taken care of, kind of privileged, and I loathe it.

"Do you not ever worry," I ask, "about being out, and exposed, and vulnerable to whatever might come along?"

"No," Howard says as he and I trade red wine and a cigarette. "'Cause I have them."

"Exactly," Tailbone adds. "I mean, two bigger assholes you'll never wanna meet. But . . . I can't imagine these days sleeping without 'em. Probably couldn't even get to sleep, I imagine. That's the truth."

"Family," Mickey says matter-of-factly.

Am I the first person ever to be envious and longing to be accepted by a gang of homeless bums?

"Is it okay for me to ask how you guys wound up . . . well, here, in this situation, in the first place?"

"Women!" all three roar, in tune, in time, and as if they have been waiting for this question forever.

I know, as I laugh, that this is a far more serious thing than it sounds. And I know, that if I probe even just a little further, that there will be no shortage of horror stories, delivered with gusto, and venom, and bile, and possibly even dollops of truth, and that none of it will be truly funny even though the soliloquy will certainly be. I know, and I laugh even harder.

I know, men blaming women and believing it. I know, and I laugh, because it sounds funny and if it's not funny, then what else is there? If it's not funny, then what is it?

The fat rain now bouncing loud off the rubber protective inflatable roof above us sounds funny, and soothing.

"So, fair trade," Mickey says. "Now, tell us how you got that cast."

Fair. Fair trade. Well, yes. These guys, yes, why not?

"He broke his arm trying to wipe his own ass, because he never had to do it before," comes the voice from above, from above the blobby bouncing raindrops.

"Stacey?" I say, leaping up reflexively because even if I

didn't recognize the voice, the words would have spoken for themselves.

I have flipped the raft straight up into the air and into the breeze. It sails back and away from us, revealing a soaked and serious and steely Stacey.

"Hi," I say.

"I knew you'd sink when I sent you away," she says, "but I didn't think you'd sink to this level."

"I haven't," I say, accomplishing what, exactly, I have no idea.

"Would you like to join us, fair lady?" Mickey asks as Howard scampers to re-collect our shelter. Tailbone just stares up at her as if she's one of those cement St. Mary statues that suddenly started weeping real tears. His open mouth should be collecting a load of fresh rainwater.

"Thank you, but no," Stacey says in that ultracool Stacey-ness that is more impressive and intimidating than anything else I have seen in my travels.

I, naturally, am up on my feet and up close to Stacey, thrilled at the very presence of her.

"You're here," I say.

"You're perceptive," she says.

"I'm sorry, Stacey, for coming by . . . your place of work, and your home and everything and being, like, a bother and all. I feel really stupid and sorry and, like, yeah . . . ."

"I didn't make it back for curfew tonight," she says, the rain running down over her face.

"Oh," I say. "Oh. Where were you?"

Tired, wet, and inconvenienced Stacey is not a person one should ask something like that.

"I'm here, right now, talking to you, under these conditions. Do you really need to start questioning stuff like that, Kiki Vandeweghe?"

Before I can offer my obvious and simple answer, Mickey takes the wheel.

"No. Nope. No way. Not at all," he says.

"You want to stay here with us?" I ask hopefully. "It's not much, but at least it's—"

"Are we a *tribe*, Kiki?" she asks firmly.

"Yeah," I say. "Yeah, absolutely."

"Are we a something, a whatever, a God-knows-what-you-were-thinking, but here we are?"

"Um, yes," I say. "Yes, absolutely."

"You do not belong here, sleeping in the rain, do you?" she says.

"No," I say, because I will say what Stacey says.

"So, do I, then? Belong here, sleeping in the rain?"

I shake my head emphatically, no.

She stands there with her arms dropped at her sides and the rain pelting the whole of her.

"Would you like to see my father's book of poetry?" I say, finally.

"Well," she says, "that sounds wonderful. But I bet you say that to all the girls."

"You know," I say, taking her hand, which feels quite specifically drenched to the bone, "you *are* all the girls."

"You're lucky," she says, allowing me to tow her along, "that the weather is in your favor and I have limited options."

"I will agree with you," I say, "that those things have left me lucky. I feel lucky."

"Yeah, well, don't go feeling all that lucky. I'm not one of those girls who feel obligated . . ."

"No obligation expected," I say. "No matter what, I already feel as lucky as I need to, and as lucky as I ever have."

All the hoots and barks and shouts of "Way to go, Kiki," and "You the man, Kiki," as Stacey and I leave the beach are probably not helping my case as a gentleman.

All the most maniacal horror movies have the twin peaks of sex and murder that make them viscerally right and wrong enough to blow your senses to smithereens.

This is exactly where my mind is at as I pull the moosehead key chain out of my pocket. Stacey is not only with me, but it was her idea. On the other hand, if I open this door and Syd is on the other side, I'm fairly certain I won't have such a great story to tell. I look behind me, as I've done a hundred times already, because I cannot shake the feeling we are being stalked. So now I'm the meat of a paranoia sandwich, with threats in front of and behind me. It's possible that smoking dope and drinking wine do not agree with me entirely.

I am hoping my lady friend cannot see my chest heaving in and out with desperation as I turn the key and burst through like I'm expecting to confront a home invasion.

Which is ironic, since we are the home invasion.

"Are you all right?" Stacey asks, putting a hand on my thumping chest, which only stokes the thumping further.

"Sure I am. Of course I am."

And when we step into the house and nobody cracks a chair over my head, I am a little more all right. I feel more nervous when I flip on the lights. It is so bright in this place. Nobody is up in these hours and if they are up, they are up to no good. I feel like the bright lights call too much attention to this bright shiny home and I am already looking forward to shutting down again.

"I suppose you'll want the tour," I say.

"I want whatever Molly got," she says slyly.

So we do the condensed version of the walk-through: living room and kitchen.

"You want food?" I ask her as we pass the fridge.

"Too tired to eat," she says. "I'll take you up on it when we get back up, though."

"Good answer," I say, and am just about to switch the light off when Stacey spies the book on top of the washer-dryer.

"Ah, here it is. Kiki's big book of seduction."

"Oh God, please don't call it that. Of all the things it is not, that's probably number one."

"Okay. I am taking it to bed, though. Which, when you think about it, means it is exactly that."

It didn't really matter what she said after the taking-to-bed part.

"Right this way," I say.

I lead her to my room, but on the way past I just have to gently try Syd's doorknob. Thankfully, still locked. I imagine what it would have been like if he was already in there and just emerged at some point. The thought makes me briefly lose all the feeling in my hands and feet.

"Charming," Stacey says as we enter my modest bedroom.

"It's home," I say.

"Mind if I use your bathroom?"

"Sure," I say, "right over there."

She is gone for less than five minutes, but it's an anguished time for me anyway. I can't decide what I should be doing. Clothes on? Clothes off? Underwear? Shorts with no shirt? Bathing suit? What's the etiquette on this kind of thing? I am well lost and panicking at the notion of failing the big exam on the first question.

"This *is* a glorious robe," she says, standing just inside the room and all inside Syd's very popular bathrobe. The book is still in her hand.

"So, you really are determined to get the full Molly," I say.

"Yup. I hope you don't mind, I hung my wet things up on the curtain rod."

"Mind?" I say. "Oh, no."

"You going to sleep like that?" she asks, pointing at my own none-too-fresh outfit.

"No," I say, but I don't do anything about it except stare at her, lovely, gleaming in that robe. Jesus, what if it's the robe? If I just fall for everybody who puts that robe on, then I think we've figured out what my freakery is.

"We didn't do anything," I blurt.

"'Scuse?"

"Molly and I. When she was here, she just slept, and showered. Wore the bathrobe for a while."

She is beaming at me and I have no clue what it means though I'm aching to find out.

"I was wondering about that," she says. "I was thinking you might have a little problem that way."

That's what it meant?

"Huh? No. No, no, no. I *could* have done it. I don't have

any problems. Well, okay, not that I don't have *any* . . . but no, not that one. I was kind of dying . . . to do it. I was way, way into it."

"So . . ."

"I thought I was doing the right thing. I thought I was acting the way a decent man should act. And I guess I believed that if I showed Molly that there were decent guys out there and not everybody was just here to use her, then . . . then . . . I don't know what."

"You thought you could, what, *repair* her? With your goodness?"

I never for a second thought of it in those terms. Until now.

The best I can manage is a shrug.

Stacey manages far, far better.

She unties the sash on the robe, disrobes, revealing herself in just her underwear and one book of poems for modesty. I have some testicular turmoil going on but at the same time there is also a form of relief, now that she has set the etiquette. I drop my clothes to the floor as quickly and awkwardly as possible, the cast on my arm suddenly deciding to fight me for the shirt. In the end, Stacey comes over and rescues me.

"You're an idiot," she says, calmly coaxing the shirt away and dropping it to the floor. "But you are a freakishly noble idiot."

She leads me over to my bed and we lie down, on our sides, pressed close together in the small space of it. I am behind her, with my casted arm draped over her. She nestles in.

"And then you did her laundry, while she slept. Remarkable."

"Not too remarkable. I like doing laundry."

"And you don't often get a chance to do ladies' undies, I imagine."

"True. But it honestly made it harder, the whole noble good-guy thing. A lot harder, actually."

Slowly, her head turns in my direction. "Seriously?"

I don't think I've given away anything there. Seriously. And now I'm squirming, physically and otherwise as she traps me in my corner.

"Um, seriously?" I stammer. "Seriously, what?"

"You did, didn't you."

"No," I say.

"Yes," she says. "You had yourself a little Molly-whack to tame the beast within."

This is about as caught as caught gets, and I don't even have the mental muscle to speak.

"You *are* a good guy. Molly's knight in gooey armor."

I close my eyes tight, wishing it all to dissolve. I hear her snap the lamp off.

I feel her shift, turn to me, and start kissing me. And

kissing me. And she is not stopping, not rolling away or anything. I am quaking with rushes of every kind.

"Can I turn the light back on?" I say.

"Must you?" she says.

"Yeah. Because I'm afraid if I don't see it, I won't believe it."

When I wake up, she's at it.

The book.

"I assume you have read all of these," she says with a thick voice and a sniff.

"No," I say, burying my face in the back of her head. I don't care about the book. I care about the back of her head. And her back. I love Stacey's back and think I might just cling to it with all I've got until the fire department has to come and remove me.

"A lot of them, anyway, right? These are some of the most—"

"Some," I say. "Though for most it's been quite a while. Growing up . . . they were a big part of everything, when I was growing up."

I'm expecting her to roll over and take me face-on on that one. To inquire forensically about the poems and their history. She doesn't, though. She flips a page. A few minutes later she flips another page. Many minutes later, another.

I hang on to her, listen to her deep breathing along with the turning of the pages. This will be my reading of the book with my face pressed to Stacey's skin, and from here it is indeed a wonderful work of art.

"I would think," she says, closing the book with a pop, "that I would read a collection like this if most of the poems were about *me*."

Ah, cripes.

"They're not about me," I say while trying to hold on to her for whatever is left of now. This painfully fine and dwindling *now.*

"How do you know, if you won't even read them?"

"It's the kind of thing a guy knows."

"Not sure I get what you mean by that," she says.

"Not sure I do, either," I say.

We go quiet again and I lie there breathing Stacey skin, absorbing Stacey molecules, seeing Stacey scenes playing on Stacey screens in my head. This is what I knew was waiting out here before I could ever know what *it* was. This is what I came for and if all the difficulty had to happen for this to happen then it has all been superb difficulty, and thanks for it.

She is reading the poems, and her lungs are shushing rhythmic responses that thrill me probably too much for anybody's comfort.

"Why are you here?" she asks.

Caught way, way off my guard, I come up with, "Do you always talk to books when you're reading them? That's intense. My lips move, but that's not even close to the same—"

"Ki-ki . . . ," she says, almost patiently, almost not, completely husky-hot.

I take her all the way seriously now, which means an extended pause, which I have no doubt she understands intuitively. I do my best to assign and assemble the constituent parts of the answer.

"Certain events put me on the road ultimately, that's undeniable. But I'm convinced that that was just about timing and I would have made the same trip eventually. Probably soon-eventually. The big answer would be that I had exhausted all the other options, belonging-wise. I never fit myself in anywhere, not really, and I suspected that further afield somewhere I would find a someplace, a somebody, a collective of somebodies—"

"A tribe."

"A tribe, who would have me and I'd want to be had." I squeeze her around the ribs and she laughs at that.

"And you think that is this, that is us? Crystal City and the Hairy Homeless? Hey, sounds like a band."

"You're not saying that thing about you having a beard again, right? Because you still do not have a beard."

"Well, no, I just meant a general kind of scruffiness but, thanks. Thanks for the reminder. By the way you still don't have one either."

"Ouch. Okay, sorry. And yeah, somewhere in the depths of my mind I think I felt like . . . I don't know. Like people in your situation were the ultimate outsiders of outsiders of outsiders. Outside of all the other insides, and so a kind of special class all your own. I think I gravitated to that."

The silence that settles over us now feels of a different type from the warming, comfortable ones earlier. I don't like it, and want to chase it away, but think I'd better wait for something instead.

"So, this is kind of like a project for you?" she says in a tone that makes even the bad silence welcome. "What are you, a Boy Scout, working toward your merit badge in *slumming*?"

Oh God, no. Every alarm screams in the fire station of my mind, and I vault right over her to land, crouching, on the floor, looking into her face. Every last syllable of my vocabulary has been checked and found to be unavailable or unqualified to put this one out. I am frantic, pulling my lips tight and shaking my head no and no and no while I take the hand she is dangling over the bedside gently between both of mine.

She still gives me a disapproving look and triggers uncontrollable forces within me that I don't truly even want to control, but my last traces of practical sense beg me to control them for the love of—

Resistance, however, is way past futile.

"I love you, Stacey."

Even I don't think that will pass over uneventfully.

She slowly turns her face away from me, but down, into the pillow. Then she takes the book, which she was holding up in her left hand, and lowers it to close up any spaces that let light or me in around the pillow's edges. She does, however, leave me holding the other, free-floating hand. It must look like a deathbed scene.

"Sorry about that," I say.

There is no audible response. The hand is still with me, though.

"You could suffocate, Stacey. And if you tell me that's what you want because of what I just said, then that will crush me. It might look cool in a memoir to have a girl commit suicide because you didn't love her, but to have one do it because you *did* would be crap."

The pillow giggles.

The heart soars.

I was making no effort at humor, but we take what gifts fall upon us.

"Don't say it again, though," she says with the unstated trade being the sight of her face again, live and lovely. She could have held out for much more for that.

"Out loud, certainly not." I can make no promise beyond that. I'm not even sure I can make that one.

She reappears and yes, as a matter of fact, I do see her even lovelier than before.

"You'll need to work on that 'out loud' part, too. But I suppose it's your own little pleasure dome up there and I can't do anything about what you do inside it."

"Magnanimous of you," I say, pulling on a pair of shorts and heading to the bathroom on a completely unrelated mission. She returns to poetry.

The shorts have been employed for under a minute before they are dropped again and I am in the shower. I feel a little funky physically from the night I had under the rain and toxins. So I leave the water a bit cool and it feels like a dream washing over me.

It was not a dream, though. I had the light on.

It feels like yet another dream, but I think I can hear Stacey reciting out loud as she reads.

Something about me, moving her like that? Some kind of sorcery. The me in that book is a special guy. I'd like to know that me, again.

He wrote about little me. About him with me. About us, my me and his me, the together me's.

Would he write about this version? This, now? Would anybody?

Those are no reasons to write a poem about me.

Stacey is a reason to write a poem about me. The one reason that could make me poem-worthy, and he doesn't even know she exists so that's that then.

I shut off the water, listen for the voice reciting, but it isn't. I towel off and put shorts on as quickly as possible because I have that flesh-eating anxiety that Stacey is going to disappear or that she never was here at all, light or no light.

I'm not far off.

"What are you doing?" I say as she hands me the bathrobe. I have folded her pants and shirt neatly and was hoping to make a goofy little presentation of them. In my wildest hope I even thought I might wash them. Maybe wash our clothes together, while we ate and watched a movie or something.

"Sorry," I say as she takes first the pants then the shirt off my hands and dresses right outside the bathroom. "I didn't get the chance for the wash-dry-fold service, so I jumped straight to the end."

"Oh God," she says. "You jumped to *the end*? You mean the end-end? Did you get ick all over my things? Should I walk myself through a car wash on the way home?"

She pokes me in the ribs and I double over with the blow of it. Not the rib-poke.

"Not exactly one we're going to be sharing with the grandkids, eh, Stacey?"

I straighten back up, disappointed and concerned over her lack of any retort.

"I'm leaving," she says with a straight face that I wish would bend one way or another.

"You're leaving?" I ask, still too surprised by this kind of thing than I should be.

"Yes, dodo. I'm leaving. Everybody leaves a place like this before too long. And anyway, I always leave. This is already too much time for me here. I leave. Then I move on. And then I leave."

I thought it sounded bad when she first said the word "leaving." But it's rapidly taking on weight and power, like an avalanche.

"Let me make you something to eat first. Then we can both leave together."

"I mean, leaving Crystal City, Kiki. I mean, really leaving."

This, now, is a five-alarm panic far worse than last night's paranoia or the worry that Syd might have been here.

"But, Stacey? What about us, and last night, and what happened and us and that stuff we did and all that. And us?"

"Wow. Are you sure there is poetry in your bloodline?"

"Aw come on, Stace. This means . . . I think you can tell this means a lot to me."

She reaches out and holds my face in her hand. "Of course I can tell. That's why I did it."

"Good. Great. Do it again, then. How 'bout now? Now's good for me."

She pulls her hand back and holds up one finger.

"One," I say. "One. One?"

"Yeah, that was it. It was lovely, but that was it."

"What? What? Why?"

"Okay, listen, if I told you in advance that I was doing you a favor because of your neediness, I don't think that would have done much for your confidence. What would you have said if I told you I was just offering you a pity bonk?"

I really don't know people at all. I would have thought the answer was already written all over me.

"What would I have said? I would have said thank you. I would have said God bless you. I would have said, sure pity me. Pity me until I cry. In fact, I'd say even if I do cry just ignore it and carry on with the pitying, regardless."

She looks at me with an expression that is undeniably pity and I don't know how I could have missed it before. Well, yes, I do know.

She gives me a big warm hug and I hang on to her as firmly as I can. "You are a very funny guy."

"Really? Did you think I was joking?"

"I think I might actually miss you. And I never miss anybody when I leave."

"So then don't. Stay here and have me all the time."

She shakes her head. We both knew that one would be a head-shaker.

"Then, take me with you."

Shake shake shake.

I feel as if I am hurtling through all the life experiences I had missed before now. Achievement and satisfaction and love and loss and resignation are all bunched up together and blurry as they whip by. Time itself, I believe, goes faster in Crystal City than it does elsewhere.

"When do you leave?" I ask her, really wanting to figure this out. "How do you know, if you just want to keep moving from place to place to place and so on, when it's time for you to go?"

Stacey stares at me in a very hard way, like she is trying to drill thought directly from her brain into mine because words always fall a little bit short. The intensity is considerable, and it feels like this is the time to look away. But I figure this is the time to hang in.

"I leave," she says in an almost angry voice but a totally honest one, "when I feel like I have saved somebody."

I stare for a good long time, trying to discern any kind of joke. Because I could not have conceived of anybody I have ever met saying this as anything but a joke. But again, I never before met anybody who would have even bothered saving anybody else, so what would I know?

I am this close, *this close*, to taunting Stacey with a question about how many people she has saved, and what, technically, constitutes a save. It seems like a good laugh for a millisecond, before I realize it would have put me this close, *this close*, to grievous bodily harm.

"Is that possible?" I ask.

"I believe it is, at least in small ways. Other people, you can save them a little, and that's something like a sense of purpose. There's the *possibility* of success in that. I believe there is. I *decided* there is."

"Well, Stacey, that sounds like a fine . . . wait a minute. Me? Is it me? You can move on now because you saved *me*? I am responsible for throttling my own heart?"

She giggles, and it's a damn refreshing sound but I don't have time for that right now.

"Stacey?"

"Well, come on, Kiki, I did save you from the horrors of that virginity of yours."

Oh. What? Wait. Oh, now.

I want to talk to Stacey about the thing I have most not wanted to talk to anyone about, ever. Why do I want to do that? Not because I think there is something in it for me, because this feeling was already bubbling up, making me want to even *search* for things that I never talked about, so I could talk about them now, with her. What is that? It's powerful, scary, way stronger than me. What is it? Why?

"Well then," I say, cartoon cool, "you can just stick around because you haven't saved anybody."

"No?" she says.

"No. You were not my first."

Her eyes go as big as Molly's. "I wasn't? Wow, I like to think I'm not easily fooled, but you got me there, big time."

"Hey," I snap, making her laugh on top of everything else. "Well then, wisegal, you'd better just brace yourself again. Because I'm pretty sure I slept with a guy."

What I am prepared for now is possibly more joke cracking, possibly a pat on the back, but certainly something demonstrative.

What I get is not at all that.

True enough, the wide wonder of the eyes I'm looking at would make Molly's look like pinholes by comparison. But the words that follow the extended pause bring another twist.

"The single most unexpectedly interesting thing you have had to say since I met you, and you hold it back until now?"

I nod and smile until it all comes together.

"Are you saying everything else was . . . *uninteresting*?"

She reaches and tugs my arm like she's ringing a church bell. "Oh, get over yourself. That's all in the past. You got coffee? Because now I want details, especially about that 'I'm pretty sure' part."

A person of real substance might feel damn cheap here, about trading on his tangled and troubled recent past like this. But you know, too bad, person of real substance.

"There is definitely coffee," I say, punchy, like I've already had nine cups of it. "Great coffee. Everything around here is always the best stuff. Probably bagels, too, who knows, let's check the freezer."

There is a light rapid-fire knocking at the front door and I get a jolt.

"More company?" Stacey says. "See, you'll be just fine without me."

"Wait, what are you doing?" I say, chasing after her.

"Answering the door."

"No, if it's my uncle, he'll string me up for having you here."

"I haven't met your uncle, but I'm betting he doesn't knock on his own door before coming inside."

"But wait," I say, too late.

Stacey opens the door wide to greet our company.

"Shit, Molly." Stacey gasps.

She gasps because it is, really, a shit Molly.

She stands there looking tiny, dirty, and electric in the eyes. From four feet away I can smell that awful cast, and now I'm wondering if there's some kind of infection or something under there. But none of that is the true shit Molly part.

The right side of her face is battered, swollen, and discolored to the point where that side of her head looks like a very low-grade roast beef.

"I see our Billy is a fucking lefty," Stacey says icily.

When Molly speaks, it comes out sounding demented and would even if the words were rational. Which they are not.

"I have never been so happy in my whole life, Stacey, so be happy for me. You're happy for me, right, Kiki? And I just came over to borrow your book. I swear I will bring it back unharmed. It's that it is *such* a beautiful book and I just know Billy is gonna love it every bit as much and he's real poetic and beautiful inside and he loves me and I'm good for him. And one of the good things I'm doing is getting these poems and reading them to him. I'll bring it back unharmed, though."

"Where is he?" Stacey says just as icily and as if she hadn't said it already.

"Please be happy for me, Stacey. He is a good man and I am good for him and we need each other and I have never been so happy in my whole life and that's the truth."

"Ah, Molly," I say, shaken up by her condition more than she seems to be.

"I said I would bring the book back unharmed, Kiki. Did you hear me when I said that? And I know Billy will get a whole lot out of it and it'll be good for him just like I am."

"This is why you didn't answer when I called you, yes?"

"I didn't know you called me," Molly says.

"Bullshit."

"I didn't, I didn't but that doesn't matter, because I am really happy now, happier than I have ever been and I just want you to be happy for me, Stacey, and I just want you to lend me that book, Kiki, which I will bring back unharmed and so if you just let me have that now I will be out of your way and you can get back to what you're doing. What are you doing, anyway? Doesn't matter. Never mind."

I see a decrepit brown people-carrier crawl up to the curb. The large bald head that swivels in our direction just has to be the Billy of infamy.

The low growl coming up from the depths of Stacey tells me she has seen him too. Molly whips around streetside and gives him a quick wave, which he does not return. Then she's back to us.

"Please hurry," she says even more desperately. "I told him I'd just be a couple of minutes and that by the time he went around the block I would be out again, and so, I'd really just like the book now, please, and we won't bother you again. Except of course to return the book. Which I promise I will do—"

"Yeah, unharmed," I say, and turn to go fetch the book.

Billy boy revs the engine a few times jackass-style, and it's almost as if the accelerator works on Molly as well. She rises up on her toes and says a much higher "Please?" as he guns it.

"You can't have it," Stacey says.

"What?" Molly practically cries it.

"Well, it's not actually published for another couple of months. But we'll be happy to put you on the notification list for when it becomes available."

"What? But he *has* it. I saw it. I read it myself and cried."

"But I borrowed that copy, and it's the only one. Sorry, girl."

"So, you lend it to me, then."

"Well, then I lent it to someone else, and jeez, you know how it is when you lend a book. Stupidest thing in the world you could ever do."

I love what Stacey is up to while at the same time hating the sight of what it's doing to Molly. The poor thing looks like she's going to dissolve bit by bit until she gets fully absorbed by the welcome mat.

Billy guns the engine. Which touches Stacey's tolerance limit.

"Hey, you!" she shouts, brushing Molly aside to do it. "Screw! How 'bout you just take off before my boyfriend here comes down there and kicks your ass."

Oh, dear God.

The visions that explode in my mind now involve me kicking nobody's ass, but Billy dragging me behind his van for a few hundred miles, then dumping me back in front of the house where my uncle has returned to find his careful quietude destroyed, which requires that he stomp me right there in front of the house and the girls and everything.

On the other hand, Stacey called me her boyfriend.

And, this being Crystal City, there is even a third hand.

That would be Billy slamming his door and marching his way up toward the house.

"Oh, shit," I say, even though I am embedded at the back, safely behind both girls.

They, however, show no signs of going anywhere. Molly stays just off Stacey's shoulder. Stacey, from my perspective, appears to be rearing up.

Jesus, she's going to fight him.

I lunge forward, grab the back of both girls' shirts, and haul them into the house. I slam, lock, and bolt the door.

He knocks, heavy, loud.

"Mol, come on, we're going," he says.

"I'll be right out," Molly calls.

"You will not be right out," Stacey says. "She will not be right out," she yells through the door.

"Mol-ly," he grunts.

"She's not coming," I say. "So, why don't you just go."

There is an extended gap, during which there are no words exchanged but we can hear Billy's breathing through the door. Clearly.

"Are you seriously telling me that this guy brought you here to get a book of *poetry*?" Stacey asks Molly.

"Yes," she says, apparently underreporting. "But I said it was my book, and I forgot it by mistake. And that I had left twenty dollars in it."

"Oh," Stacey and I say in unison, "right."

"Do you have twenty dollars," I ask, "y'know, for when he eventually came looking for it?"

"No. But don't you see, by then we would have the poetry, and it wouldn't matter."

"Oh Lord . . ." Stacey huffs at her.

When even the breathing goes away, I move over to the living-room window to see what's happening.

"Damn," I say.

"What?" Stacey says.

"He's in his car. Waiting us out."

"I'll just call the cops, then," she says.

This time it's Molly and me in unison. "No."

Molly's rationale is apparent. Mine, not quite so.

"What's up with you?" Stacey asks me.

"I don't want to bring the cops here. We just can't."

Stacey grins devilishly.

"Just how much of a desperado is this uncle of yours? I can't wait to meet him."

"God*dammit,*" I say when I look back out the window.

"Stacey, could you use your remarkably powerful powers on something more helpful?"

"What? I did nothing. If this is erection-related—"

"My uncle. You made him appear. He's just getting out of a cab. I'm screwed now."

"Ah, what could happen?" she says.

"I don't even want to think about it," I say.

I watch him get out, then walk around the front of Billy's van while staring fiercely at both Billy and the van. For his part, Billy stares right back then returns to staring up here. At Syd's house.

Syd walks around the front of the van and stands on the curb by the driver's-side headlight with his arms folded. After several seconds of this, Syd makes an unmistakable gesture indicating Billy should move on.

Billy does not heed the advice.

So, slowly, Syd unfolds his arms, walks directly up to the driver's-side window and therefore the driver, and gets very, very close to him.

Then, Syd steps back, to the sound of tires screeching and that engine racing, fortunately away this time.

"Go, Syd!" I say, proud and pumped up. "He took care of Billy."

"Yeah," Stacey says. Molly goes all silent.

I watch Syd approach the house.

I watch *Syd approach the house!*

"C'mon, c'mon, c'mon," I say, hustling the girls toward the back door.

"Why?" Stacey says.

"Because he'll throw me out. He's dead serious about his privacy and his rules and if he catches me messing with them, I'm out. I'll be friggin' *homeless*," I say, and actually expect sympathy.

"Oh, you poor sonofabitch," Stacey says as I scoot them out the back door.

"I'm sorry," I say. "Just that way, across the field. I'll meet you at the beach later, right? Right?" When neither one answers, I answer myself and hope for the best. "Right."

I close the door, reverse course, and see Uncle Sydney walking through the door at the same time I come across his bathrobe on the floor where I dropped it at Molly's knocking.

"Hey, Uncle Sydney," I say cheerily as I snag the robe and duck into the bathroom.

"Hey, Kevin," he says, just as cheerily and probably not like the voice he used a few minutes before. "You gonna be long in there? I'm bursting."

"Me too," I say not entirely untruthfully but in a different way. "But for you, I'll be quick."

And I'm true to my word. I hang the robe in the closet, flush the toilet, and come out.

"Are you back a little early?" I say.

That seems to rub him the wrong way. "No I'm not," he says. "Whenever I come home is the time I'm supposed to come home." He squints at me as he passes on his way into the bathroom. It's not a nice look, but I'm hoping it's because he has to go so bad.

RUDE AWAKENING

When I opened my eyes, reluctantly, I was in Jasper's bed.

I stared at the ceiling, blinking, blinking, wondering, figuring, hoping, blinking, wondering. I could tell indirectly, from the abundant ambient light, that it was a bright, sunny day. I could tell also that when I had to address that fine brilliant day more head-on, it would mean many types of pain.

Only when I spied all of my clothes on the floor a few feet away did I notice the absence of any clothes on my body.

Only when I probed very carefully around the bed's surface area with one hand did I conclude that I was here alone. And only then did I sense it had been a while since I'd exhaled.

I exhaled. I was relieved to be alone, and that was no criticism of anybody who might have been there.

Jasper had been extremely kind to me. Thanks to the

varieties of darkness I now realize dark rum can produce, I'm not 100 percent certain how far that kindness went. I might not be 60 percent certain.

I'm not certain I want to be certain.

I needed him last night, and he was there. Right now I didn't feel like I could face him. Not yet.

I jumped up out of bed.

I got immediately so dizzy and flushed I had to lurch to the dresser and steady myself with both hands. That left me leaning and looking right into Jasper's mirror and my sad, strange mug, which caused me to shove right off again before I would have to punch that face. I got to my things and with as much focus and dread as possible, gathered my clothes in some arrangement over me, and slung backpack over shoulder before exiting, slipping out of the bedroom.

I was like a reverse burglar, creeping down the hall with a loot bag, trying to get away without any valuables, but trying not to be seen by any of the home's occupants, either.

As I was about to pass the kitchen door, I heard stirrings in there. I smelled coffee, heard the rustling of bags, and composed a picture in my head of doughnuts and fresh orange juice and, goodness, that coffee was smelling good. Dunkin' Donuts, I reminded myself, Dunkin' Donuts, the taste is always a disappointment compared to the aroma.

That wasn't the deciding factor in getting me to then

bend low and hope for the best as I scurried like a big rat right past the kitchen door toward the exit. I caught a break. He must have been facing the other way or into the fridge because there was not a word of protest as I made it to the front door and silently got myself out.

I felt even more like a rat out in the light of day, but I couldn't handle talking to Jasper yet. And because he was Jasper, I suppose I was counting on him to do all the understanding for both of us for now.

TIME RETALIATES

I run out of both hope and wine money more or less simultaneously.

The beach has become my center of operations more than Syd's place. I've put in hours there, killing time and then resuscitating it again every time I thought I caught a glimpse of either Stacey or Molly. I've been to the hostel, where neither of them is a resident anymore, and the bus station, the beach again, up and down pointless shitty streets, back to the beach again. Pathetically, I even spent yesterday afternoon staking out the shop where we got those subs, my veal Parm and their meatballs and steak.

The moment is right now, though, when I realize I will probably never see them again. I am ashamed at the childish sadness I am feeling for the absence of two people I met not even two weeks ago. It's a picture-perfect summer evening here on the shore of the wastewater of Crystal Beach and what more could a guy want?

If I could tell them good-bye, even. And thanks. Even that.

"Hey, man, no, no, come on now," Mickey is saying, patting my back. It seems I've failed at bravely masking my melancholy. "These things happen all the time, to all of us. It's all temporary, man, all of it. Hell, see how recently I met you? You're already, like, my fourth oldest friendship that is still currently up and running."

I do manage a laugh at the thought, though looking closely it's not a funny notion at all. What is a funny notion, however, is that Howard and Tailbone seem to believe they've got the raft properly fixed, sealed, and filled and are heading down to the water for a twilight test launch.

"Possibility of success, zero," I say as they hit the water.

"Yeah, but possibility of damn entertaining failure is very high," he says.

So the two of us drag on down to the good seats near the shore, buoyed on the hope of entertaining failure.

Mickey knows I'm mooning around over the girls because I haven't been able to shut my sad mouth over it. But there's another thing getting at me that he doesn't know and couldn't know, because I only know it myself as of right now when I open my mouth to release it.

"I miss my dad," I say, watching the guys pull away toward the horizon with their flimsy plywood paddles.

"I don't miss mine," he says.

"That's because you're smarter than I am," I say.

"Did I imagine it, or did you tell me lately that he's the one who broke your arm?"

"Did I say that?"

"I think so. Somebody did anyway, so I'd say it was most likely you."

"Yeah," I say. "Anyway, yeah. I miss him."

"How long you have to wear that thing on your arm anyway?"

"I figure I'll hang on to it until there's no room left for any more signatures, then I'll get it removed and give it to a museum, as a memento of my adventures."

"If I was you I'd give it to my father, as a memento of *his* adventures."

"Huh. I like the way you think, there, Mick."

"Ah, yup, there we go," Mickey says, pointing out to where the guys are now flailing around madly trying to turn the clearly distressed rubber vessel back to shore.

"Ha," I say, and the situation deteriorates rapidly to the point where it is now just two guys with plywood planks hacking around at the water without any apparent purpose. Many of the denizens of Crystal Beach have come running—

well, no, not running, but an accelerated version of the limpy, shuffly thing they ordinarily do—to hoot and laugh and shout wildly inappropriate sailor innuendo at the two entertaining failures as they wash up.

It is fine comedy, and the closest I've seen yet to a widespread communal moment among the beach's fragmented population.

"Awesome, guys," Mickey says as the boys approach.

"Seriously," I add. "Great show."

"We do it again at nine tonight," Tailbone says with a wheeze and a salute.

"And two-thirty matinees on weekends for the kiddies," Howard adds.

They pass us by, heading up to dry off and spark up as usual.

"What were we saying again?" Mickey asks. "Were we finished?"

"Yeah, we were," I say, and we follow the spark.

But times are lean, and it is about the time I would be shelling out for some wine. However, I am nearly out of shells. It's not great news to the guys, but also not a situation they find unfamiliar.

"Yeah," Mickey says solemnly, "we're all running pretty low about now."

I quickly discover how certain topics will turn certain

guys from chilled out to worked up without much warning.

"Not him, though," Howard says to Mickey while pointing angrily in my direction. "Come on, man, lookit him. He's not broke. He don't know broke or nothing *about* broke."

"Come on, Kiki," Tailbone says, "are you holding out? Don't hold out on us, man. It's us. We're your boys, your family."

"I know that. If I had money, I would hand it over, just like I have been."

Of course I have *some* money. Everybody has some money, but that doesn't mean they're not broke. Wine money is one kind of money and I'm all out of that. Whatever little bit I may have stashed back in my room is a whole different thing, and it's there for a reason, for when I'm really stuck. The fact that I have no money here now means I am broke. Somehow I'm not sure I could accurately get that idea across very well in this situation.

"Right," Mickey says, "we just have to go on a quick fundraiser, is all."

"A fundraiser," I say warily.

"It's a blast, you'll love it."

Because I am the rookie, the unmade man of the group, I am required to wear the gang's big tattered old backpack and serve as the beast of burden for the expedition.

"We're going *in* there?" I say as we come up through the bushes off the canal path, a little uncomfortably close to Syd's place.

"We?" Mickey says. "Well, no, not me. I'll be watching the house from the back. Tailbone will be out front. Because this is Howard's scout, and he's been in the place before, you two are going in."

"I used to boff a chick that lived there. I was snagging stuff out of that house the whole time, even when I was an invited guest, and I don't think anybody ever noticed. They got a big summer house someplace and they're away all this month. I been watchin'. This is a great neighborhood, a really great neighborhood. Okay, there, rookie, it's gonna be no different than shopping."

As I crouch down with everybody else looking up at the house, I grip my thighs hard to stop my hands from shaking and letting on how shitless scared I am.

"Shopping," I say. "Sure, I know how to do that."

"Yeah," Howard says, "I'm sure you do."

I am sure of only one thing at this moment and that is that I wish I were anyplace else on earth. What am I doing? Is this me, now? Is this what I do and how I'm going to live? I'm completely terrified, in addition to not having any rational explanation for why I am here.

"You're a straight-up guy, Kiki," Mickey says as he gets up

to take his position. He gives me a hug. "I know you're scared, and you probably don't even need to do this. That's huge to me, to us, and nobody's gonna forget it. Stuff like this, it's for *life*, man, you know what I'm sayin'?"

"I think I do, yeah," I say.

I *fear* that I do, is what I honestly should say.

"Remember, emergency situation with no warning, if somebody's coming from the front, Tailbone yells "Front!" and you haul ass out back. If they're coming from the back, I holler and you shoot the other way."

"What if it's front and back?" I ask.

"Well, in that case, obviously you're boned, my friend."

"But, if he does get caught," Tailbone says, "he's the only one who could convince them that he's the owner of the place." He punches my shoulder and heads to his post.

"Right," Howard says as he produces a heart-stoppingly big flick knife and easily works the feeble lock off the bulkhead door. "The whole thing shouldn't take ten minutes. I'm grabbing the small valuables like jewelry and shit, and I'm pounding all the bigger stuff, electronics, bigger silver and gold items and whatnot straight into your pack. You are simply a dumb transport animal, so don't try and make any decisions on your own, got it?"

"Got it," I say, and I cringe at the trembly weakness of my voice.

He hears it too. "Don't you shit the bed on me here, Kiki, all right?"

"I won't," I say, feeling the terror people must feel as they are about to skydive for the first time.

"Go," he says, and we are off.

We shuffle through the dark basement, lucky that it is largely empty. Howard steers me quickly to the staircase and we feel it wobble as we go up. We enter the kitchen and immediately he starts pushing things, a hand blender, a crystal decanter, into my pack. Dining room, he pulls me to a stop at the sideboard and I shudder at the loud sound of him pouring silverware on top of the other things.

Living room, a brass carriage clock and a notebook computer sitting on an end table.

Up the stairs we go, hitting a bedroom, emptying out a three-story jewelry box that I cannot see the contents of but the cascade of stuff sounds expensive enough. He takes extra time, pulling me back when I wrongly guess we are moving on. He's doing some selecting back there, jamming particular items into the pouches of his carpenter's belt rather than dumping them on me. There is a second bedroom, which has a tall men's wardrobe that makes Howard gasp with ecstasy when he sees a collection of two dozen glittering fine watches on an inside shelf all displayed on a tall tube like a man's arm. He works like a squirrel as he shifts and sorts and stuffs three out of every four of them into his own pouches and the rest into mine.

There is a second, bigger laptop on one of the bedroom night tables and then a small tablet computer on the other. Those get jammed into my bag, complete with power cords, and I can feel it's taking some packing now to get it all in. The weight is considerable at this point, and when he pushes down my knees buckle, though they would probably be buckling from the fear by now without any extra weight at all.

"Isn't this enough?" I ask.

"Shut up," he says. "It's never enough. Why else would we be here? There is one more bedroom, and we are going there."

I sigh, and comply.

It is clearly a young girl's bedroom, all ponies, pastels, and boy bands on every wall.

"There won't be anything in here," I say. "Let's go."

"What did I tell you, man? You are just labor here, I am the decider."

He goes tearing through the little girl's room, thrashing around much more viciously than the other rooms. "I hate this pink shit," he growls. "*Hate* it." He tears all the covers off the bed, picks up a cartoon-cat alarm clock, and pitches it against a wall, breaking the clock and that piece of wall at once. "These brats are totally spoiled today, so there has to be some ridiculous expensive electronic crap around here someplace."

"She probably took it to the summer house," I say, pleading for this kid I know nothing about.

"Lookit this," he says, pointing to the child's desk. "Who has a fat-ass computer like this anymore? What is she, a lousy kid, they don't waste the good stuff on her? Bet she's a damn *dummy*," he says, flipping the whole setup onto the floor as he does it. "Stupid, stupid little bitch," he says, while I just put as much space between us as I dare.

"Whoa-hoo there," he says, going to the spot where the computer was and pulling up a big envelope that was taped there.

"What?" I say, as he leers into the envelope. He comes and shows me what's inside.

It's cards and smaller envelopes, savings bonds and large-denomination cash notes. The stuff of birthdays and holidays and old relatives with experiences and successes investing in young ones to someday have the same.

"Howard, no," I say.

"*What?*"

"We can't take that."

He makes a squinting, munched-up face that I take to mean I am mentally defective.

"Right, Kiki, we break into a house and do a robbery, but

we don't take *this*? Yeah, we got scruples, we'll take all your shit, but we draw the line at cash money because really we're good guys at heart."

"Yeah," I say, "but it's more than just—"

"Shut up, I mean it. What's the little slut gonna do with it anyway except splash these weedy little wet-dream assholes all over her walls, and they can't even sing, by the way."

"That's it for me," I say. "I'm done."

I'm three strides toward done when he grabs my pack and yanks me toward him again. "You're not done till I say you're done, Kiki." He is still towing me toward the farthest corner of the room and the closet, when I nearly topple over backward from the weight and the pulling. "Having a sudden attack of superiority, is that right, pal? You really believe you can keep your head above that line because you are participating in *almost* an entire B&E? Go ahead and try to tell that tale to people who don't have to do this kinda shit to survive. Tell them your story, how you only stole a *lot* of stuff from somebody's house but you wouldn't steal some *other* stuff. Do that, and then see how many folks think that makes you one of them, on that side of the line, and not one of us, on this one."

I am too weak now to fight, physically or otherwise, and I just stand like the pack animal I am.

"Just get on with it, will you?" I say wearily.

"That's more like it," he says, opening the closet.

I have to listen again as he spits more hateful filth over the shoes and bags and dresses that he hurls across the room. But it ends when he hums with satisfaction, and then I hear the familiar jingle of coins, a fat-bellied lot of coins. I look over my shoulder just as the pink porcelain piggy bank comes up, and down again, pushed, stuffed, squeezed into the pack, which has no room for it, and which now weighs one whole more me.

I feel like a two-legged newborn colt trying to manage the trip down the stairs. Howard, who is turning out to be a finer teammate every minute, is playfully and unhelpfully pushing and pulling from behind making it a lot more treacherous.

There are still maybe ten stairs to go when we hear Mickey shout, "Back! Coming from the back!" and that's all.

"Holy shit," Howard says, and I don't even get a chance to contribute anything at all before I feel the overwhelming shove riding on the back of the gravity that had already been working on me. I'm pitched forward, both arms outstretched like Superman, only nothing at all like Superman and my elbows crash and my ribs take an almighty crunching as Howard tramples right over the back of me and bombs forward and out the front door.

I am in a heap and in pain in eight places as I thrash

and writhe my way through insane panic and the convoluted strappings of the old, overstuffed backpack. It feels like hours I'm struggling to escape and I can hear things crackling and snapping among the merchandise. I am sad and sorry for that because none of it is mine to break and who the fuck am I, anyway? Though I can't see or hear anybody at all, I have the overwhelming feeling that I am being observed in this most horrific moment of my sorry, sorry life. There is a thickening of the air over my final struggles to break away. It's nearly bringing tears of humiliation and definitely bringing asthmatic wheezings of panic.

The backpack simply won't let me go. I burst up and away, still lugging the sea-monster bag full of all those things that do belong here, and I bolt for the door because I do not and knew that all along, and shame on me for that, for everything.

I am at the door already when I realize that in my freaking I ran the wrong way. At the minute I simply do not care, and outside is all that matters, so I go right on and shoot out that back door, through these people's modest little backyard. I still don't sense anybody anywhere and I'd keep running even if I did. Through the hedge into the dense greenery growing next to the lazy slow canal that I know is just another short way ahead. I smell it, and am overcome that I can.

HELLO GOOD-BYE

Hangover and confusion fermented into rage during the sweaty stomp between Jasper's house and Dad's. By the time I walked through the door, I was totally toxic, so his decision—for the first time since I had arrived here—to come rushing to greet me at the door was an unfortunate one.

"Kevin!" he called, like exactly the way I imagined the scene to play out when I first *chose* his house, his life, his company, over everybody else's. "I have been dying to—"

I shoved him right aside, and into the hall tree full of jackets, and kept on my way. As he bumbled and stumbled around I went directly to the breakfast bar, pulled the shiny, sturdy, stainless-steel laptop out of my bag, and tested its ruggedness by slamming it down hard.

"What are you doing?" he said, coming after me.

I had very little idea what I was doing.

"I don't want that thing," I said. "You'll put it to good use, I'm sure."

He grabbed me from behind as I was heading for my room. I spun around, glared at his hand on my shoulder, and he removed it.

There he was, standing in his pale blue shirt and his dark blue tie and the beginnings of his sweat stains blooming already at the armpits. Every bit the big-deal, small-town, perpetually perspiring high school principal heading for the last day of the school year and all the summer thrills he couldn't wait to start spanking on.

"Please?" he said weakly, holding the laptop and pushing it on me. "Do keep it. And get yourself cleaned up and ready and we'll ride in together. We'll talk."

"What will we talk about? Peru?"

He said nothing, but his down and up and side-to-side eyes said Peru to me.

"Fuck you. I'm done with your school, and with you," I shouted, and turned again toward my bedroom.

He grabbed me again. He grabbed me, again. On the worst morning for grabbing ever.

I wheeled around on him, and with every ounce of raging resentment flowing through me I swung the looping punch straight for my father's lying mouth.

I was already thrilling on the terrified eyes of him when he brought up the armored laptop just in time to block the hardest punch I will ever throw.

"Shiiiiiiiit!" I screamed, dropping right down to my knees and wrapping my left hand around my right wrist because if I didn't, it felt like it would just break up and fall to the floor in a bony bloody mess.

We were sitting in another waiting room, after emergency, after exam, after X-ray confirmed the broken bone in my wrist caused by my feeble idea of a punch. The doctor said it was a very small fracture in one of the very small bones of the wrist. It was borderline whether a cast was needed, and often patients opt for just a splint or even an ace bandage.

We were waiting to get my cast fitted. I figured I had earned this cast. If they had offered to plant a little flag in it like on a moon landing, I would have gone for that, too.

"Remember how great we were before?" Dad said, cutting a long silence to shreds.

"Don't," I said.

"Do you remember us, Kevin-Eleven?"

"I still have one healthy hand. And elbows and feet and knees if necessary," I said.

We sank back into silence until a very long time later

when I got called in finally to get casted up. I think we were both relieved to be separated just then.

In fact, I know we were.

"He left this for you," the receptionist nurse said when she finally noticed the little boy with the cast looking all around for his father.

Inside the envelope there was a sticky note, a bank card, and not very much money.

The note: *Had to get to the school. Withdraw some cash (PIN: 1396). Take a cab. Get some rest. Wait there for me. Love.*

The coward.

I got the cash, the maximum daily limit. Went home, sat in a bath with my arm hanging over the side. I dressed, packed a few things, added my bit of saved money to my father's generous contribution.

I left his bank card on top of the laptop on top of the breakfast bar, and walked out of the place I did not belong, to find the place I did.

THE WAGES OF SIN

I can only imagine what I look, smell, and sound like when I get my breathing only partway under control prior to putting that blessed key into that forgiving lock.

And I don't want to imagine it. I just want to be inside, bury this bag of booty in my closet until I can be rid of it somehow, and have a shower. I am going to wash as much of this shameful shit off me as I can and start learning to live with the rest. So, I *belonged* for a few minutes there. Is that what I was looking for? Belonging to *that,* to *them*? Trading in whatever better self I possessed for that honor?

I turn to shut the door on all that and leave it outside.

"Just get in, *in,*" Howard says in an urgent whisper. He has his big fuck-off flick knife pressed right at my navel as he backs me in and closes the door behind him.

"Here," I say, panicky, trying once more to wriggle out of the backpack. "Just take it all, man, and go. I don't want my cut at all."

He is leering at me sickeningly as he uses the scary sharp knife to slice through the pack's straps like they were string cheese. The pack thumps to the floor. There is no way the real man of the house does not hear this, even if he's napping.

"Your cut? Shithead, there is no *your* cut. There never was. God, you're a fuckin' chump. How you likin' hangin' with the underclasses now, sweetie?" He gives me a shove toward the kitchen and follows behind me.

I can smell that sometime earlier Syd was doing something nice with garlic and pork and I think cider vinegar. That would have been a time and a place to be. Would have been exactly the time and the place to be.

Right down the block from the stupid shit I was doing.

As we pass, it catches my eye that Syd's bedroom door is open. It's never open.

Just inside the kitchen, Howard gestures to the back door, where in the panel of tempered glass, my humiliation is multiplied by the sight of Mickey and Tailbone laughing at me.

"Go let them in," Howard says, and immediately begins his well-practiced prowl through somebody else's home.

I open the back door at the new lowest point of my life.

"Nothing personal," Mickey says in a manner that makes

it sound almost true. They have just stepped inside when a wall-shaking commotion kicks off in another room.

I freeze, and more important the other two do as well. We wait, through the crashing and banging, one great bellow of fury, and another howl of terror and pain.

Then, Howard comes staggering backward into our view, falling on his back across the threshold between kitchen and hallway. His own big flick knife is sticking up out of his abdomen as all the blood and life of him pours out of his completely motionless body.

Tailbone and Mickey, the other members of Howard's "family," nearly knock each other out in the scrum to get through the back door and away from it all first. The words "honor" and "thieves" swirl circles around each other in my mind.

I feel panic in the most tangible way. I think of the train that I never heard, running past Jasper's house, as I try to slow my locomotive breathing.

Syd appears, stepping over Dead Howard after looking close enough to confirm he was Dead Howard.

His words to me are cool, but I am only too aware how much effort it is taking him to maintain it. "It's one of my unbreakable rules, Kevin, that a person who enters my house with a knife in his hand, leaves it with that knife in his gut."

"Good rule," I try to say, but it's only whispers because

my vocal cords have been shocked into rigidity. I clear my throat. "What do we do now?"

"Well, *you* are going to try not to touch anything more than what you have to while you pack up your things."

The fact that I will be moving on again comes as neither a shock nor a disappointment.

"Can I have a shower first?" I ask. "I'm kind of rank."

"Sure," he says, "we're not barbarians, after all."

The numbness I feel is almost peaceful, though it makes the shower a strange sensation. I don't quite get the tactile feel of the water pit-patting my skin, but clean is coming and that's the sensation I really need.

There's a dead guy in the kitchen. A *person*. Not a *good* person, but a somebody. A somebody I knew and spent time with and who talked, and who's never going to talk again. I can't believe I am here, that I'm in a place where people get killed. Jasper never killed anybody when I was at *his* place.

Jasper's place. That would be a nice place to be now.

"What the hell is this?" Syd barks as I step out of the bathroom. I can all but hear the tough fibrous muscles of my heart tear wide open with the fright.

"Jesus, Uncle Sydney," I say, holding on to the wall with one hand and my chest with the other.

"Sorry, Kev, a little abrupt there, should have given you warning. But for chrissake, *poetry*?"

"Yeah, right?"

"He's published a book of *poems*?"

This could take a good while for Syd to wrap his head around. To Syd, this kind of strange, artistic behavior registers more than murder, apparently, which is one more excellent reminder that I need to get out of here rapidly.

"That would appear to be so, yes."

"Did you know he was into this weird shit?"

This leap has got to be like interplanetary travel as far as my father's brother is concerned, but I cannot be his guide through it.

"I knew, some. I knew he wrote. The collection, though, came as a surprise to me. What can I say, Syd?" I shrug as dramatically as I can.

"I shouldn't be surprised, though. He always had poetry written all over him, the freak. How did it get here?"

Ah. That.

"Came in the mail, Syd."

"The mail. Huh. So the bastard did know you were here."

"The bastard did, it seems."

He hands me the copy of *Mind Monkeys*, shaking his head sadly. I head to my room to add it to my already packed bag.

"Hey," he calls, summoning me back.

I walk apprehensively to where he's still standing in front of the bathroom.

"Did you wear my bathrobe? The thick, soft, white one that hangs in the bathroom closet? Because it smells funny."

How is it that this small question can bring my heartbeat thundering back up as high as anything else that's happened lately?

"Um, uh, sorry, Syd . . ."

"Did I forget to tell you not to touch my bathrobe?"

"Honestly, Syd, I think you forgot. Because if you ever told me something like that, I'd never have done it." I become acutely aware I am talking to a killer. A killer who is not happy with me.

He nods calmly at me. "It smells girly funny. Are you a freak, too?"

About three different times I feel like I am about to give an answer but it stalls out each time.

"Can I get back to you on that?" I ask.

He turns and walks toward his bedroom.

"No, you cannot," he says.

When we meet again a few minutes later, Syd is sitting at the kitchen table, drinking coffee, eating an avocado with a spoon, and staring with contempt at Howard the dead mess on his floor.

"Can I ask you one last thing?" I ask, standing over him as he looks up with a wry expression.

"I'm listening."

I hold out my arm, with the cast. "Could you cut this off for me? I don't think I need it anymore."

He gets up, goes to the deep kitchen drawer, the bottom one that holds all the mad miscellany. Then he comes at me with a tool that looks like the missing link between wire cutters and bolt cutters.

"Wow," I say as he buzzes up the plaster from elbow to palm as if he is filleting a tender fish. "That is some serious implement."

"Yes," he says with a flourish as he makes the final cut and the cast drops to the floor without much of a thud at all. "It's a quality thing. And you would be surprised at how many useful applications it has."

I am flexing my muscles, opening and closing my fist, marveling at how skinny my forearm looks, when he stands up, reaches over me, and tucks the cutters down into my pack.

"Thanks," I say, standing up with him.

"That's your going-away present. Every man should have one of them things anyway."

"I meant thanks for everything, Syd. I'm sorry if I let you down."

This, the point where he could let me down easy and lessen my unease? He nods, instead.

"So, what are you going to do about this?" I say, gesturing at Dead Howard at the same time my uncle starts rather firmly ushering me to, and then through, the back entrance.

"Take care of yourself, Kevin. You're a good kid, in spite of it all. Go and live the life you're supposed to, whatever it is and wherever it is."

"Thanks, Syd, I will," I say, shaking his hand with my newly freed hand.

"And that map I gave you, of how to get here?"

"Yup?"

"Lose it."

The door closes.

FAMILY EXTENDED

Two blocks clear of Syd's house, as I am expecting the world to begin its descent to something I might recognize as normal, Molly comes bouncing toward me from the opposite direction.

"But I just want to borrow it. Just that one book, just for a little while. And I'll bring it back and it will be completely unharmed."

"Wow," I say, standing still to greet her.

"Wow, yes, wow," she says, hopping like a grinning pogo stick before me.

My heart hurts when I see how my presence brightens her up. Like I, or the book, can make things in any way better for her. But what do I know? Maybe she's right. Maybe the book is right.

Her relentless try-for-happy game is almost working. She

looks no better than the last time I saw her. And her cast positively reeks.

"So," she says, "can I borrow it? Can I?"

The first thing I think to do is put all kinds of conditions on it, like how she needs to do this and that and stay away from that one, and blah blah.

All of it unenforceable, unfair, and none of my business. I can wish her luck, but I cannot force it on her.

However, I know what I can do.

"No," I say.

She all but melts into a puddle right there on the sidewalk. "No? But, Kiki, you—"

"No, I won't loan it, but I will give it to you, on one condition." I hold up my arm.

"You're out!" She squeals. "That's terrific."

"Yes it is," I say. "Terrific. I feel like a new person. And I would like you to have that feeling."

"What?" She looks closely at her toxic friend there on her arm. "But I *need* this."

"Well, sure, that's up to you. I think you don't, but . . ." I take off my backpack, fish out the book, and as soon as she sees it she starts a childlike moan like she badly needs to go to the bathroom and everybody else is opening up Christmas presents without her at the same time. I then pull my new surgical tool out of the bag.

"Do it, hurry, do it, hurry," she says, looking away.

I do not miss my chance. I sit her down on the curb, take a seat beside her, and slice through the cast even more quickly than mine came off.

"Holy fish, Molly," I say as the fumes come up and burn my eyes shut and cauterize the linings of my sinuses.

When I look again, she is on her feet, with the book in one hand and the no-longer-broken arm in the air. She is staring at it, wiggling her fingers and flexing just like I did. I stand up, and she immediately kisses me on the cheek without even looking.

"Thank you for everything," she says, backing away.

"Thank you, too. But, slow down, slow down. Where's Stacey?"

Molly's getting miffed with the delay. She snorts, then blurts, "I escaped. From Stacey. She was not letting me out or do anything I so chose to do. I mean, she means well and does have honorable intentions, but, she's a little crazy, I think."

"Is that what you think?"

"Yes, she's like a cult, actually, and I simply had to escape, to get away from her. Now, I told you, and so can I please take my book and go? It's going to be so important for me and for everybody. Please, Kiki?"

I find my gaze drifting up, from her big shiny eyes up to her big shiny Cleveland Browns helmet of hair, the one indestructible constant throughout all this. Then, in a shift at once subtle and alarming, she steps back and looks at me with an expression of shocking, comprehensive sanity.

"And tell Stacey thank you for me, too. Will you? Tell her I love her and appreciate her and value everything she tried to do for me. And then tell her that I don't need saving. Tell her I don't want to be saved."

Still caught up in the wind rush of that change, I take a couple more ticks to catch up.

"Sure, Molly," I say. "Of course, if I get the chance, I'll tell her."

Once more she smiles big and unfocuses those fluid eyes—almost like it's a choice—and backs up into her Molly-ness for good.

"I can't wait," she says, clutching her book hard. "This is going to be a beautiful turn of things, a turn for beautiful things." She's bouncing and bobbing, in a huge rush now to get to the place she is in such a hurry to get to. She is glancing equally, though, between the book and the arm. I choose to see this as a hopeful thing.

She is still thank you, thank you-ing as her voice fades off down the road.

I am back down, returning the cutters to the bag and closing up shop.

"She only thinks she escaped," Stacey says.

I jump up, surprised for a flicker, then not. "Going to walk me to the bus station?" I ask.

"I'd be honored," she says.

We walk, we talk, and sadness builds in me with each step. But indecision, no. Regret, no.

"So, did you earn that merit badge?" she asks.

"About twelve times over," I say.

She takes my hand. "I can remove your cast before I go," I say. "I'm licensed now."

"No. I'll wait until I'm healed, thanks."

"Sensible as always."

"That's me. I believe you owe me a story, don't you? I have a vague memory about something you think you might have done but weren't sure? We were cut off before you could finish."

"There was no finish. Probably won't ever be one."

We are almost to the bus station.

"I'm going home, Stacey. There are people there for me. And I have to deal with them."

"Good boy," she says.

"You could come with me, you know. I mean it. I would love that."

We are in front of the shiny glass doors that we came through to start this whole thing. She shakes her head gently, heartbreakingly, and unnecessarily.

"You go," she says. "You do belong somewhere after all, and it sure isn't Crystal City. There's no shame in actually belonging someplace. Any one of us would go back if we had that. Go."

"I'm going, I'm going," I say. "What are you going to do?"

I hate sad smiles. They are a perversion of everything I will ever understand. She sees me staring and probably pouting and she looks down for a moment. Then she comes back up with a smile less sad, less sincere, less Stacey.

"I am going to wave," she says, and as I try to come closer to her she takes one crisp step away from me, and starts waving.

She is still waving when I go through those doors, and when I look back over my shoulder a few seconds later and a few seconds later.

I look for her when the bus pulls out of the depot, hoping she will still be there to wave me off from the once-in-a-lifetime summer holiday to paradise.

She's not there anymore. I wave to her anyway. I'll probably never stop.

CHRIS LYNCH is the Printz Honor–winning author of several highly acclaimed young adult novels, including *Inexcusable,* which was a National Book Award Finalist and the recipient of six starred reviews. He is also the author of *Freewill, Gold Dust, Gypsy Davey, Iceman,* and *Shadow Boxer,* all ALA Best Books for Young Adults, as well as *Little Blue Lies, Pieces, Kill Switch, Angry Young Man, Hothouse, Extreme Elvin, Whitechurch,* and *All the Old Haunts*. Chris teaches in the creative writing MFA program at Lesley University in Cambridge, Massachusetts. He divides his time between Boston and Scotland.